NEW PENGUIN SHAKESPEARE

GENERAL EDITOR: T. J. B. SPENCER

ASSOCIATE EDITOR: STANLEY WELLS

WILLIAM SHAKESPEARE

*

AS YOU LIKE IT

EDITED BY
H. J. OLIVER

PENGUIN BOOKS

PENGUIN BOOKS

Published by the Penguin Group
Penguin Books Ltd, 27 Wrights Lane, London W8 5TZ, England
Penguin Putnam Inc., 375 Hudson Street, New York, New York 10014, USA
Penguin Books Australia Ltd, Ringwood, Victoria, Australia
Penguin Books Canada Ltd, 10 Alcorn Avenue, Toronto, Ontario, Canada M4V 3B2
Penguin Books (NZ) Ltd, Private Bag 102902, NSMC Auckland, New Zealand

Penguin Books Ltd, Registered Offices: Harmondsworth, Middlesex, England

This edition first published in Penguin Books 1968
Reprinted with revised Further Reading 1996
28

Printed in England by Clays Ltd, St Ives plc
Set in Monotype Ehrhardt

CONTENTS

INTRODUCTION

As You Like It is one of the plays in the Shakespeare canon of which it would be easy to give a completely misleading account – and to give it not by inventing what is not there but merely by stressing selected features rather than others. By some such method, one could even argue that this was an unsophisticated play.

What, for example, could be more blatant than the exposition: 'As I remember, Adam, it was upon this fashion bequeathed me by will, but poor a thousand crowns, and, as thou sayest, charged my brother on his blessing to breed me well'? (One even wonders whether Sheridan had this in mind in *The Critic* when Dangle complains that Sir Walter Raleigh, in Puff's dreadful play, is telling Sir Christopher Hatton what Hatton already knows: 'Mr Puff, as he *knows* all this, why does Sir Walter go on telling him?' – to which Puff replies ' 'Fore Gad, now, that is one of the most ungrateful observations I ever heard – for the less inducement he has to tell all this, the more I think you ought to be oblig'd to him; for I am sure you'd know nothing of the matter without it'.) And as if Orlando's speech were not exposition enough, there soon follows Oliver's cross-examination of the wrestler Charles, including the obviously 'unnatural' and, at the time, irrelevant question 'Can you tell if Rosalind, the Duke's daughter, be banished with her father?' Only in the 'Romances' of his last years was Shakespeare quite as casual as this.

What, similarly, could be more unsophisticated than the

unashamed melodrama of the snake and the lioness from which Orlando rescues his brother Oliver – 'natural' dangers no less unnatural in the Forest of Arden, in Warwickshire, than they would be in the Forest of the Ardennes in France? What could be more melodramatic than the earlier character of Oliver, so villainous that he proposes to burn the lodging where Orlando customarily lies, and burn it with Orlando inside it? What could be more improbable than the conversion to goodness of this same Oliver –

> *'Twas I, but 'tis not I: I do not shame*
> *To tell you what I was, since my conversion*
> *So sweetly tastes, being the thing I am –*

converted because his brother saved him from the lioness? Only, surely, the conversion of the wicked usurping Duke, converted to the religious life because he met and had 'some question' with an 'old religious man' (V.4.151–62) – while advancing with an army

> *to take*
> *His brother here and put him to the sword.*

But just as the man confident in his truth can afford to joke, so Shakespeare, when the important things he has to say are most subtle, can be most casual about his method of saying other things; he gets them said and, as it were, out of the way. Writing, probably, in 1599, with the experience of many comedies behind him (including not only *The Two Gentlemen of Verona*, *Love's Labour's Lost*, and *The Taming of the Shrew* but also *A Midsummer Night's Dream*, *The Merry Wives of Windsor*, and perhaps even *Much Ado About Nothing*), he is already master of his technique and, as Mackail once put it, writes with 'relaxed art'; because the mere story of the play is relatively unimportant, he gives it little attention and concentrates on his lovers and his pastoral theme. Moreover, the play that in many eyes is still the best statement in English literature of that pastoral theme, of the beauties of life free from 'painted pomp' and far from the madding crowd, proves to be anything but simple statement: it may be the finest pastoral drama in English but it is also the most amusing comment on those works of earlier and Elizabethan literature that began and ended with the premise that the country life,

exempt from public haunt,
Finds tongues in trees, books in the running brooks,
Sermons in stones, and good in everything.

Shakespeare's immediate source was just such a work, the one that Thomas Lodge wrote 'to beguile the time with labour' on a voyage to the Canaries, *Rosalynde* (or *Euphues' Golden Legacy*), published in 1590. This in turn was based on the medieval *Tale of Gamelyn*, which was once ascribed to Chaucer and even appeared in editions of *The Canterbury Tales*. *Rosalynde* is a true pastoral, in a mode very popular during the 1580s and for years afterwards, and still enjoyed by modern readers in the poetry of Spenser's *Shepherd's Calendar*, in plays such as Fletcher's *The Faithful Shepherdess* and Ben Jonson's unfinished *The Sad Shepherd*, and in Sir Philip Sidney's *Arcadia*. *Rosalynde* is set, theoretically, in the woods of the Ardennes (curiously placed somewhere between Bordeaux and Lyons, the latter being on the way to Germany and so to Italy!), but in practice these are Arcadian lands and resemble neither French woods nor any others of human experience. Lodge's characters, both the noble lords and ladies – like Rosader and Saladyne (Orlando and Oliver), Rosalynde and Alinda (Celia) – and the shepherds and shepherdesses

– like Montanus (Silvius) and Phoebe – are little better than conventional types. Their life is unreal, their conversation artificial and, indeed, mostly Euphuistic; and the story of their loves is told ostensibly to point the moral

> *that such as neglect their fathers' precepts, incur much prejudice; that division in nature, as it is a blemish in nurture, so 'tis a breach of good fortunes; that virtue is not measured by birth but by action; that younger brethren, though inferior in years, yet may be superior to honours; that concord is the sweetest conclusion, and amity betwixt brothers more forceable than fortune.*

Presumably no reader believed a word of it, or was intended to believe it, but it is all completely delightful, and not least so for its pretence that sensible men and women, given the choice, would live under the greenwood tree. Or, as Lodge's Coridon expresses it:

> *For a shepherd's life, O Mistress, did you but live a while in their content, you would say the court were rather a place of sorrow than of solace. Here, Mistress, shall not Fortune thwart you but in mean misfortunes, as the loss of a few sheep, which, as it breeds no beggary, so it can be no extreme prejudice: the next year may mend all with a fresh increase. Envy stirs not us; we covet not to climb; our desires mount not above our degrees, nor our thoughts above our fortunes. Care cannot harbour in our cottages, nor do our homely couches know broken slumbers: as we exceed not in diet, so we have enough to satisfy: and, Mistress, I have so much Latin,* Satis est quod sufficit.

Rosalynde, in short, was a notable example of what we have learned to call 'escapist literature'.

Shakespeare was fully sensitive to the charm of Lodge's romance; he could also see its unreality. The greatness of

As You Like It is – if one may risk so pretentious a statement – that he retained, and enhanced, the charming artifice of his original and at the same time smilingly revealed its conventionality and unreality.

He retained the charm of *Rosalynde* – and perhaps met what seems to have been a demand for plays on Robin Hood and similar subjects – by taking over both Lodge's basic story (although he omitted all the violent deaths) and its setting (although the European woods of the Ardennes perhaps became conflated with his own Warwickshire Forest of Arden). His banished king, Rosalind's father, 'is already in the Forest of Arden, and a many merry men with him; and there they live like the old Robin Hood of England: they say many young gentlemen flock to him every day, and fleet the time carelessly as they did in the golden world'. The Duke (unlike the banished king in *Rosalynde* in this) duly expounds the pastoral philosophy – so well that his phrases have become proverbial:

Now my co-mates and brothers in exile,
Hath not old custom made this life more sweet
Than that of painted pomp? Are not these woods
More free from peril than the envious court?
Here feel we not the penalty of Adam,
The seasons' difference . . .?
Sweet are the uses of adversity,
Which, like the toad, ugly and venomous,
Wears yet a precious jewel in his head;
And this our life, exempt from public haunt,
Finds tongues in trees, books in the running brooks,
Sermons in stones, and good in everything

and Amiens adds 'I would not change it'. As soon as they have the chance, however, they do change it: the Duke, hearing that his brother has become converted to a religious life and has abandoned all claims to the crown and lands, waits only to complete the nuptial ceremonies before going back to the envious court, to 'the good of our returned fortune'. And his co-mates and brothers in exile are apparently just as ready to abandon their pastoral principles – with one notable exception, Jaques.

It is significant that in Lodge's romance there was no character corresponding to Jaques. Shakespeare created him, and created him, obviously, for a function similar to that of Mercutio in *Romeo and Juliet*: not to 'debunk' romance, so that there was nothing to be said for it, but to cast the eye of a likeable cynic on romance, and, in *As You Like It*, on pastoralism and other such 'romantic' convention as well, so that the audience, seeing from more than one point of view, could smile and tolerate. Jaques, in fact, is Shakespeare's main method of keeping romanticism and pastoralism in their place.

This function is not confined to the conclusion of the play, when Jaques alone remains true to the philosophy 'Sweet are the uses of adversity' and refuses to engage in mere 'pastime': his place is now with the converted Duke, who in his turn has 'thrown into neglect the pompous court', with the further advantage for Jaques that

out of these convertites
There is much matter to be heard and learned.

In exactly the same way Jaques has previously tried to show up the shallowness of the greenwood philosophy, and to the song

Who doth ambition shun,
And loves to live i'th'sun,
Seeking the food he eats,
And pleased with what he gets:

Come hither, come hither, come hither.
Here shall he see
No enemy
But winter and rough weather

he has added a third stanza:

If it do come to pass
That any man turn ass,
Leaving his wealth and ease,
A stubborn will to please:
Ducdame, ducdame, ducdame.
Here shall he see
Gross fools as he,
An if he will come to me. II.5.47–54

He has not only affirmed what the exiled Duke has himself suspected, that for exiled courtiers to live on venison is all very well, except that it is rather hard on the deer –

And, in that kind, swears you do more usurp
Than doth your brother that hath banished you –

but has also pointed out that Orlando does mar the trees 'with writing love-songs in their barks'; that Touchstone's country wife will soon lose her charms; and that a joke can go too far. Hence the important scene (III.3) of his interference when Touchstone proposes to perpetrate matrimony with Audrey in unseemly haste:

And will you, being a man of your breeding, be married under a bush like a beggar? Get you to church, and have a good priest that can tell you what marriage is. This fellow will but join you together as they join wainscot; then one of you will prove a shrunk panel and, like green timber, warp, warp.

It is a curious reading of the play that prefers to sentiments such as these Touchstone's lame answer: 'he is not like to marry me well; and not being well married, it will be a good excuse for me hereafter to leave my wife'; and one wonders how many misreadings of the play derive from such an unwillingness to give Jaques his due.

To give him his due, however, is not to give him the last word, and it is certainly not to consider him Shakespeare's mouthpiece or 'chorus'. In particular it is unfortunate that his famous 'seven ages of man' speech is so often quoted as if it expressed Shakespeare's philosophy of life, and that an admirable one. The speech is a variation on another well-known theme, and it is not Shakespeare's only variation on that theme; but just as Antonio's lines in *The Merchant of Venice* –

> *I hold the world but as the world, Gratiano,*
> *A stage, where every man must play a part,*
> *And mine a sad one –* I.1.77–9

express his particular melancholy, and Macbeth's lines –

> *Out, out, brief candle!*
> *Life's but a walking shadow, a poor player*
> *That struts and frets his hour upon the stage*
> *And then is heard no more. It is a tale*
> *Told by an idiot, full of sound and fury,*
> *Signifying nothing –* V.5.23–8

express the depths of his acquired despair, so Jaques's lines give one impression of human life – according to which the only significant thing about a baby is its 'mewling and puking'; honour or reputation is a 'bubble'; justices are creatures overfed (probably on food given as bribes) and cannot rise above platitudes; and old age is 'second childishness' and complete forgetfulness. As many a commentator has noted, if Shakespeare's opinion is expressed at all, it is by bringing on the stage at this moment Adam – an old man whose courage and loyalty completely contradict what Jaques has just said. If Shakespeare had chosen to speak in his own person, then, on the theme of what is thought to have been the motto of the Globe Theatre ('*totus mundus agit histrionem*', from Petronius), it is reasonably certain that he would have written something different again from Jaques's speech, or Antonio's, or Macbeth's.

Accordingly we shall not, if we are wise, equate Jaques with the chorus or accept him as an oracle; we shall not join George Sand who, in her version of the play, married him off to Celia (describing this as 'my own romance inserted in that of Shakespeare . . . I have always tenderly loved Jacques'); we shall allow the cynic his cynicism and recognize with the Duke that it is probably the cynicism of the rake reformed and one who takes rather too much pleasure in his chiding of others. But we shall not therefore brand him the 'malcontent type' (though he may have something in common with other cynical commentators in plays written at this time). We shall not say that he is inevitably worsted in argument with Orlando and Rosalind, but shall recognize that he holds his own with them in the art of insult, playing a game of which they all understand the rules, and in the process scoring many a good hit ('Nay then, God buy you, an you talk in blank verse'). We shall probably put aside theories that he is in the play for purposes of personal satire – of Ben Jonson or Jonson's enemy John Marston or anybody else of whose self-confident railing his lines occasionally remind us – and maintain for one thing that he is essentially too likeable, and too often right in his opinions, to be meant as a caricature of anybody. Above all, we shall not think of him as a 'man seeking wisdom by abjuring its first principles' but shall insist that, even if he parades the fashionable melancholy, he is often wise, and that he too is a touchstone – not least when he is serving as a touchstone for Touchstone himself.

It is by no means certain that Shakespeare meant 'Touchstone' to be the name of the character so known to modern readers and theatregoers. In the early scenes in which the character appears, he is dubbed 'Clown'; 'Touchstone' first occurs in the curious stage direction at the beginning of Act II, scene 4, '*Enter Rosalind for Ganimed, Celia for Aliena, and Clowne, alias Touchstone*'. This may mean either that Touchstone was intended as the clown's name all the time or that Touchstone is the name he assumes in the forest. There is no proof, however, that the clown assumes any disguise in the forest; we learn that he there wears the motley of the professional fool or court jester, but jesting seems to be his profession from the beginning, even when Rosalind and Celia call him a 'natural' in I.2 and 'a clownish fool' in I.3.

Whatever his name, one of his roles in the Forest of Arden is indubitably that of the 'touchstone' – the stone on which alloys were rubbed, to test their quality or their degree of genuineness, and so, figuratively, the test or criterion of the genuineness of anything. Accordingly, when in Act III, scene 2, Corin sings the praises of the shepherd's life (in words clearly derived from Coridon's in *Rosalynde* – quoted on page 10)

> *Sir, I am a true labourer: I earn that I eat, get that I wear, owe no man hate, envy no man's happiness, glad of other men's good, content with my harm; and the greatest of my pride is to see my ewes graze and my lambs suck*

the words have a different effect from Lodge's, not only

because of Touchstone's reply 'That is another simple sin in you, to bring the ewes and the rams together and to offer to get your living by the copulation of cattle' but also because Touchstone a few minutes earlier has given Corin his assessment of the shepherd's occupation:

Truly, shepherd, in respect of itself, it is a good life; but in respect that it is a shepherd's life, it is naught. In respect that it is solitary, I like it very well; but in respect that it is private, it is a very vile life. Now in respect it is in the fields, it pleaseth me well; but in respect it is not in the court, it is tedious. As it is a spare life, look you, it fits my humour well; but as there is no more plenty in it, it goes much against my stomach.

In passages like these, one can see how far Shakespeare has developed the dramatic function of his fool. In the early romantic comedy *The Two Gentlemen of Verona*, the jester Speed may occasionally make a comment on the main story that helps to keep that story in perspective, such as

O excellent device! Was there ever heard a better,
That my master, being scribe, to himself should write the
letter? II.1.128–9

(and if anything the effect of the comment is *too* damaging, in that it makes the romantic hero look foolish), but for most of the time the jesting is strictly irrelevant and is there only for its own sake. In *As You Like It*, however, Touchstone's jests, like those of Jaques, are for the most part closely related to the main themes, on which they give us yet another point of view; and if only William Cartwright had seen this relevance, he could hardly have written in his 1647 verses to John Fletcher:

Shakespeare to thee was dull whose best jest lies
I'the ladies' questions, and the fool's replies;
Old-fashioned wit, which walked from town to town,
In turned hose, which our fathers called the clown,
Whose wit our nice times would obsceneness call.

The technique was to be developed even further, of course, in the Fool in *King Lear*.

It has often been said that the characters of Shakespeare's fools changed about the time of *As You Like It* because Robert Armin had joined the company to play these parts, his skill being in a more intellectual and perhaps semi-pathetic kind of humour than the skill of his predecessor, the famous comedian William Kemp. In fact Touchstone is not as different from earlier Shakespearian fools as some have claimed (and Armin records that he, like Kemp, played the part of Dogberry); moreover Touchstone's singing is confined to a few bars, although Armin was an excellent singer. *As You Like It* may well have preceded Armin's arrival by a few months (in 1600, according to the title page of *Fool upon Fool*, Armin was still playing at the Curtain); *Twelfth Night* no doubt came after it, and it may well be that this was why some of the songs were transferred from Viola to Feste.

What is certain is that Touchstone, like Jaques, has the function of casting a cynical eye on romanticism run riot, even when Rosalind herself is at fault ('You have said; but whether wisely or no, let the forest judge'); yet he does not have the last word either, and Jaques, for one, is always there to keep *him* in his place:

for thy loving voyage
Is but for two months victualled.

Shakespeare's method, then, may be called theme and

variations – unless one prefers to call it point counterpoint. Perhaps it is seen even more clearly in his treatment of the rustic inhabitants of Arden. He took over from Lodge the conventional pretty shepherdess, Phoebe, disdainful of her lover Montanus, and he remembered Rosalynde's rebuke of her coyness:

> *What, Shepherdess, so fair and so cruel? . . . Because thou art beautiful, be not so coy: as there is nothing more fair, so there is nothing more fading . . . be ruled by me, love while thou art young, lest thou be disdained when thou art old. Beauty nor time cannot be recalled, and if thou love, like of Montanus: for as his desires are many, so his deserts are great.*

But, using the very metaphor Lodge's Phoebe had used to Montanus, 'if your market may be made nowhere else, home again, for your mart is at the fairest', he transformed Rosalynde's mild rebuke into the stinging lines in which Rosalind censures Phebe (III.5.35–9, 57–60):

> *Who might be your mother,*
> *That you insult, exult and all at once*
> *Over the wretched? What, though you have no beauty –*
> *As, by my faith, I see no more in you*
> *Than without candle may go dark to bed . . .*
> *. . . mistress, know yourself; down on your knees*
> *And thank heaven, fasting, for a good man's love!*
> *For I must tell you friendly in your ear,*
> *Sell when you can, you are not for all markets.*

The pastoral love-game is not, after all, as admirable or as amiable as it had been made to seem; and the object of the swain's devotion is herself just as far from the ideal: *her* 'touch' is not so 'sweet', but she has

> *a leathern hand,*
> *A freestone-coloured hand; I verily did think*
> *That her old gloves were on, but 'twas her hands;*
> *She has a housewife's hand – but that's no matter.*

To add yet another variation, Shakespeare invented a 'real' country girl – Audrey – watching (so much for romance!) her *goats*, and ignorant even of the word 'poetical' ('Is it honest in deed and word? Is it a true thing?'). She is only too willing to abandon her country lover, and marry – Touchstone; and her ideals do not rise above 'I am not a slut, though I thank the gods I am foul'.

The rustic swain of Lodge's *Rosalynde*, Montanus, is taken over by Shakespeare as Silvius, similarly sighing for, and victimized by, his Phebe; but whereas in Lodge 'it amazed both Aliena and Ganimede to see the resolution of his loves: so that they pitied his passions and commended his patience', Shakespeare's Rosalind tells us exactly what the status of such pining lovers is: 'I see love hath made thee a tame snake'. And as Audrey is to Phebe, so William is to Silvius: the country boor as Shakespeare probably knew him only too well, set against the shepherd of literature; and William's cross-examination by Touchstone (in Act V, scene 1) leaves the country man only his simple honesty. It is vaguely reminiscent of the cross-examination of another dull William – the Latin 'lesson' in *The Merry Wives of Windsor* (IV.1) – and it is the descendant of many a wit-bout between professional jester and natural fool in earlier Shakespeare and other Elizabethan comedy, such as the meetings of Speed and Launce in *The Two Gentlemen of Verona* (for example, II.5 and III.1.276 ff.). Again the difference is that the earlier quibbling ('Well, your old vice still: mistake the word') has been transformed into an exchange that develops the theme of the play. Perhaps nobody was ever further from understanding *As You Like It* than the commentator who regretted the sub-plot of Silvius and Phebe but allowed it because it 'enhances the pastoral and woodland element' and said that the episode of Touchstone and Audrey should have been omitted because it is 'disagreeable' and not in the true pastoral spirit – unless it be the commentator who argued that Jaques was not in the play as originally written, because he has nothing to do with the plot.

One character whom Shakespeare did not need to develop much from her original in Lodge is his Celia, based on Lodge's Alinda (each taking the greenwood name 'Aliena'). Already in the prose romance Alinda is a staunch friend, treating Rosalynde as an equal (although Rosalynde goes to the Forest as her page, not her brother, and in Lodge Alinda too is banished, but not before she has told her father that she is determined to share Rosalynde's exile); already too she is an amused commentator on any undue solemnity in love. In *As You Like It*, of course, one of her functions is to laugh even at Rosalind if, exceptionally, that normally gay heroine threatens to take herself too seriously; and where Lodge's Alinda says to Rosalynde–Ganimede 'I pray you, if your robes were off, what metal are you made of that you are so satirical against women? Is it not a foul bird defiles the own nest?', Shakespeare's Celia, in a slightly different context, is even franker: 'You have simply misused our sex in your love-prate. We must have your doublet and hose plucked over your head, and show the world what the bird hath done to her own nest.' To Rosalind's claim that her affection 'hath an unknown bottom, like the Bay of Portugal', Celia retorts 'Or rather, bottomless, that as fast as you pour affection in, it runs out'; and to the perhaps only half-serious 'I'll tell thee,

Aliena, I cannot be out of the sight of Orlando: I'll go find a shadow and sigh till he come', she gives the only right answer, 'And I'll sleep'.

Not the least of the tributes to be paid to Shakespeare's portrait of Rosalind is that she is not overshadowed by this pert cousin. One reason for this, though not the main one, is that Shakespeare was not willing to give Celia the same proportion of his time as Lodge gave to Alinda, particularly as the story drew closer to its end. In *Rosalynde*, Aliena (Celia) is rescued by Saladyne (Oliver) from a band of outlaws who were attempting to carry her and Rosalynde off and had already wounded Rosader (Orlando); this naturally leads her to look on her rescuer 'with favour', and Saladyne is in turn impressed by her. Or, in Lodge's unsmiling words:

> *Saladyne hearing this shepherdess speak so wisely began more narrowly to pry into her perfection, and to survey all her lineaments with a curious insight; so long dallying in the flame of her beauty that to his cost he found her to be most excellent: for Love, that lurked in all these broils to have a blow or two, seeing the parties at the gaze, encountered them both with such a veny that the stroke pierced to the heart so deep as it could never after be razed out.*

Perhaps because Shakespeare did not wish to give minor characters an equal prominence; perhaps because he had already written a comedy in which a heroine was rescued from a band of outlaws (*The Two Gentlemen of Verona*) – and had vowed never to try it again (Quiller-Couch was to compare Shakespeare's outlaws with Gilbert and Sullivan's Pirates of Penzance and say that the difference was that Gilbert meant his to be funny); probably because the tone of the play demanded that even these romantic lovers must not be taken too seriously, he abandoned Lodge's story, risked the charge of inadequate motivation, and gave us instead Rosalind's delightful:

> *... there was never anything so sudden but the fight of two rams, and Caesar's thrasonical brag of 'I came, saw, and overcame'. For your brother and my sister no sooner met but they looked; no sooner looked but they loved; no sooner loved but they sighed; no sooner sighed but they asked one another the reason; no sooner knew the reason but they sought the remedy: and in these degrees have they made a pair of stairs to marriage which they will climb incontinent or else be incontinent before marriage. They are in the very wrath of love and they will together; clubs cannot part them.*

It is obvious that Rosalind in turn is a touchstone for Celia. She is, of course, much more than that; and indeed it has been claimed that *As You Like It* is one of only four Shakespeare plays in which the woman has the leading part. (The others are said to be *Cymbeline, The Merchant of Venice,* and *All's Well That Ends Well* – though some of us might wish to add *Romeo and Juliet* or *Antony and Cleopatra.*) He would not ask too much of the boy apprentices who had to play the female roles, capable as those boys must have been; and one of the most fascinating aspects of *As You Like It* is the skill with which even the part of Rosalind is kept within the compass of the boy actor – who can more easily play the part of a girl who for much of the time is disguised as a youth (Ganymede), even though 'she' is sometimes 'pretending' to be a girl! To the modern actress, as George Bernard Shaw has said, the role is 'what Hamlet is to the actor – a part in which, reasonable presentability being granted, failure is hardly possible'.

The Rosalind of the early scenes is a dignified and reserved young lady, as befits one who has been allowed to stay in her uncle's court, with a doubtful status, after that uncle has banished her father and usurped the dukedom. She may try in all goodwill to 'forget the condition of' her own 'estate' and rejoice in Celia's, but obviously the task is difficult, and it is Celia rather than Rosalind who bandies wit with the clown (Touchstone) on his first appearance. The pompous absurdity of Le Beau, however, draws Rosalind out; and she is the first to cry 'Alas' in pity of the old man whose sons have been badly hurt by Charles the wrestler.

The tone of her first exchange of words with Orlando (I.2) is best shown by the terms of address chosen: '*Young man*, have you challenged Charles the wrestler?'; 'Do, *young sir*, your reputation shall not therefore be misprized'; 'Now Hercules be thy speed, *young man*!' The boy actor would have no difficulty here or with the restraint of 'the little strength that I have, I would it were with you'. Then to Orlando's success in the wrestling is added another claim to Rosalind's attention – that his father, Sir Rowland de Boys, was beloved of her father (this being another of Shakespeare's additions to Lodge) – and her growing interest is shown by a simple gesture, when she presents him with a chain she had worn round her neck:

Gentleman,
Wear this for me – one out of suits with fortune,
That could give more but that her hand lacks means.

A small textual point best illustrates the difficulty that some commentators have had with Shakespeare's presentation of his heroine thereafter. In the next scene (I.3), Rosalind's depression has deepened, and Celia again tries to cheer her: 'Why cousin, why Rosalind, Cupid have mercy, not a word?', only to be told 'Not one to throw at a dog'. Then to Celia's later question 'But is all this for your father?' the reply, as given in the text of the First Folio, is 'No, some of it is for my childes Father' – that is, Rosalind's concern is not all for her banished father; some of it is for the man she would wish to be the father of any child she may have. It is a remark that Shakespeare could have written for any one of his many heroines who combine with a true modesty a frankness that refuses to beat around the bush once feelings are known to be genuine (which is not to say that Middleton Murry was correct when he rashly wrote: 'Rosaline, Portia, Beatrice, Rosalind – it is hard to recollect them apart'). Shakespeare's first editor, Rowe, however, presumably found the remark unmaidenly, and emended it to 'No, some of it is for my father's child' – a reading that was followed by Pope and most of the eighteenth- and nineteenth-century editors (Theobald being a notable exception) and duly approved by Coleridge, who complained of the Folio text: 'This is putting a very indelicate anticipation in the mouth of Rosalind, without reason; not to speak of the strangeness of the phrase'. Most modern editors find no strangeness in the phrase and prefer a frank (and not 'indelicate') Rosalind, in love at first sight, to one too much concerned about her own griefs; and they note that Shakespeare would not follow Lodge in having his heroine begin by toying with the hero.

If the Folio text is preserved, some of the comments of the 'Victorian' editors are seen to be very wide of the mark indeed. One example may suffice, Hudson's: 'Rosalind's . . . occasional freedoms of speech are manifestly intended as part of her disguise, and spring from the feeling that it is far less indelicate to go a little out of her character, in order to prevent any suspicion of her sex, than it would be to hazard such a suspicion by keeping strictly within her character'. One rewrites Shakespeare at one's peril! His conception of ideal love is neither prudish nor sentimental; like Swift, he would presumably have refused to identify felicity with 'the possession of being well deceived'.

The scene that begins with discussion of the 'child's father' ends with Rosalind's banishment. The second part of the scene, however, is in verse; and Rosalind's speeches are dignified, simple (both in sentence-construction and in vocabulary), and free from rhetoric, so that the audience is in no doubt who is in the right: the Duke is completely unable to answer the direct plea

I do beseech your grace,
Let me the knowledge of my fault bear with me.

Thereafter, until the last scene of all that ends this strange eventful history, Rosalind is in disguise – and the actor's problem is largely that of suggesting the feminine modesty, and the occasional timidity, beneath the playful exterior: 'I could find in my heart to disgrace my man's apparel, and to cry like a woman'. The playfulness presumably presented no problem to the pert Elizabethan boy; it certainly presents none to an actress (and one remembers with some amusement the film critics of the 1930s who so solemnly rebuked Elisabeth Bergner for enjoying herself so much in the part). The key phrase could be said to be 'Come, woo me, woo me: for now I am in a holiday humour, and like enough to consent'. Once Orlando has been identified as the writer of the bad sonnets on trees, and once the first misgivings have passed ('Alas the day, what shall I do with my doublet and hose?'), he is sure to be mercilessly teased by this gay young lady; it has been well said that Shakespeare's Rosalind is 'a sort of universal image of Woman as Sweetheart'. It is, then,

Rosalind who speaks the famous epigram 'men are April when they woo, December when they wed'; and it is Rosalind who pricks the bubble of the traditional story of tragic love:

> *The poor world is almost six thousand years old, and in all this time there was not any man died in his own person, videlicet, in a love-cause. Troilus had his brains dashed out with a Grecian club, yet he did what he could to die before, and he is one of the patterns of love. Leander, he would have lived many a fair year though Hero had turned nun, if it had not been for a hot midsummer night: for, good youth, he went but forth to wash him in the Hellespont and being taken with the cramp was drowned, and the foolish chroniclers of that age found it was 'Hero of Sestos'. But these are all lies; men have died from time to time and worms have eaten them, but not for love.*

Indeed, Shakespeare would seem to have gone further and to have laughed at his own earlier concept of the romantic hero. Valentine in *The Two Gentlemen of Verona* is known to be in love by, and apparently not considered less admirable for, the traditional gestures of the sighing male:

VALENTINE *Why, how know you that I am in love?*
SPEED *Marry, by these special marks: first, you have learned, like Sir Proteus, to wreathe your arms like a malcontent; to relish a love-song, like a robin-redbreast; to walk alone, like one that had the pestilence; to sigh, like a schoolboy that had lost his A.B.C.; to weep, like a young wench that had buried her grandam; to fast, like one that takes diet; to watch, like one that fears robbing; to speak puling, like a beggar at Hallowmas. You were wont, when you laughed, to crow like a cock; when you walked, to walk like one of*

the lions; when you fasted, it was presently after dinner; when you looked sadly, it was for want of money. And now you are metamorphosed with a mistress, that, when I look on you, I can hardly think you my master.

II.1.15–28

Orlando, on the other hand, is mocked for *not* having the 'marks' by which Rosalind has been 'taught' to know a man in love:

A lean cheek, which you have not; a blue eye and sunken, which you have not; an unquestionable spirit, which you have not; a beard neglected, which you have not – but I pardon you for that, for simply your having in beard is a younger brother's revenue. Then your hose should be ungartered, your bonnet unbanded, your sleeve unbuttoned, your shoe untied, and everything about you demonstrating a careless desolation. But you are no such man: you are rather point-device in your accoutrements, as loving yourself, than seeming the lover of any other.

The heroine is completely in charge of the situation and of the action of the play; it is Rosalind, needless to say, who extorts the necessary promises from all concerned, so that the right knots can be tied, or untied, at the end, and every Jack may have his Jill; and it can only be Rosalind who must speak the epilogue.

Perhaps it is the actor who plays Orlando who has the more difficult task; indeed more than one producer has thought that Orlando was the perfect 'part for a stick'. M. R. Ridley has stated the difficulty as being that 'Orlando in Arden suffers from that air of doubtless excusable fatuity that is liable to envelop the best of men when they fall in love'; and various commentators have endeavoured, as it were, to strengthen the part, in various ways. Some have seen topical allusion or even personal portraiture in it and have suggested that the interest of the Elizabethan audience in the character could have been heightened by their recognizing in it comment on a man 'in the public eye'. C. J. Sisson, for example, once advanced the theory that in Orlando Shakespeare was glancing at the real-life story of Thomas Lodge himself, who in 1593 was involved in a lawsuit concerning shares in his father's estate (but on the evidence given it is hard to believe that the resemblance would have been apparent); J. W. Draper thought Shakespeare was retelling the story of 'Belted Will' Howard and writing the play as a plea for the restoration to him of his ancestral estates (but the alleged connexion with the family of de Boys is not nearly enough to justify so curious a reading). Sir Arthur Quiller-Couch went further, and in a different direction: he thought the play could be read – and presumably that the part ought to be played – to imply that Orlando recognized Rosalind all the time. Oddly enough, he did not quote the few lines that might conceivably give support to his theory.

These are in Act V, scene 2, when the various lovers are proclaiming their virtues as lovers ('And so am I for Phebe', 'And I for Ganymede', 'And I for Rosalind', 'And I for no woman'), modulating into Phebe's 'If this be so, why blame you me to love you?' (presumably to Rosalind); Silvius's 'If this be so, why blame you me to love you?' (presumably to Phebe); and Orlando's 'If this be so, why blame you me to love you?' – which so startles Rosalind that she asks quickly 'Why do you speak too "Why blame you me to love you?"' only to be told 'To her that is not here, nor doth not hear'. Rosalind lets it go with 'Pray you no more of this, 'tis like the howling of Irish wolves against the moon'; and perhaps we must let it go too, on the supposition either that Orlando's reply is sincere or that he is for the minute embarrassing 'Ganymede' by carrying on the Rosalind pretence in public. We must let it go because the alternative is to believe that Shakespeare cheated us and cheated himself. If he had wished even to leave open the possibility of Orlando's having recognized Rosalind in disguise, he could surely not have made the Duke say

> *I do remember in this shepherd boy*
> *Some lively touches of my daughter's favour*

and have made Orlando rule the possibility out with

> *My lord, the first time that I ever saw him*
> *Methought he was a brother to your daughter.*
> *But, my good lord, this boy is forest-born,*
> *And hath been tutored in the rudiments*
> *Of many desperate studies by his uncle.*

(Nor is it necessary to believe that Oliver has learnt the truth 'between Acts IV and V'. When in Act V, scene 2, he replies to Rosalind's 'God save you, brother' with 'And you, fair sister', it is in Orlando's presence and immediately after Orlando has said 'Here comes my Rosalind'; Oliver is fitting into the spirit of the accepted pretence that Ganymede is Rosalind, both here and at IV.3.179.)

Modern audiences, and commentators, can hardly be blamed for feeling uncomfortable about this convention that a character in a play cannot be recognized in disguise, and indeed some of Shakespeare's contemporaries were unhappy about it. The intellectual George Chapman, for example, may even have been thinking of *As You Like It*, among other plays, when he had a character in his *May-Day* (1601) say to one who was contemplating the donning of disguise to solve a problem:

Out upon't, that disguise [a friar] is worn threadbare upon every stage, and so much villainy committed under that habit that 'tis grown as suspicious as the vilest. . . . For though it be the stale refuge of miserable poets by a change of a hat or a cloak to alter the whole state of a comedy, so as the father must not know his own child, forsooth, nor the wife her husband, yet you must not think they do in earnest carry it away so; . . . and therefore unless your disguise be such that your face bear as great a part in it as the rest, the rest is nothing.

Disguise, however, was a convention, and Shakespeare did not break through it.

His solution to the problem of the part of Orlando, if it is a problem, seems to have been different. In a theatre the most important impression of a character may be the first one; and, conceivably because Shakespeare thought it possible that Orlando would seem weak in the later parts of the play, he has put all the initial emphasis on Orlando's strength. Perhaps this is why he risked the obviousness of the exposition – because he wanted to open the play with the hero's justifiable complaints and determination that he will 'no longer endure it'. He then gives Orlando all the better of the quarrel with Oliver, both morally and physically; and, of course, the stress is on Orlando's manliness and valour in the scene of the wrestling. (Shaw said he always enjoyed watching this scene in the theatre – because it is easier to find somebody who can wrestle than somebody who can act!) Nor is Orlando's courage allowed to drop out of sight; if it turns out to be unnecessary, it is none the less *there* when he demands of the exiled Duke food for Adam; and it is still there when he saves Oliver from that fearsome lioness. Although this last incident is merely reported by Oliver to Rosalind, and to the audience, already the actor playing Orlando has had adequate material to work with, and need not be completely outshone even by his heavenly Rosalind.

The characterization, then, is all that it ought to be and, allowing for the difference between 'history' and comedy, should not be regarded as inferior to that of, say, *Henry IV*, probably written at much the same time or a little earlier. Examination of the 'style' of *As You Like It* similarly suggests the skill of the mature and practised playwright.

Somewhat surprisingly to some readers, much of the play is in prose. Verse is frequently used: for example, in the scene in which the usurping Duke dismisses Orlando and that in which he banishes Rosalind; in the scenes involving the banished Duke in the Forest of Arden; in the Silvius–Phebe interludes; and for Oliver's announcement that Orlando has been wounded by the lioness – in short, for the more formal or solemn parts of the play. Nearly all the Rosalind–Celia–Orlando section, however, is in prose, as befits a light-hearted comedy.

The prose is more artfully balanced and formal than one might think on first reading or first hearing it. Phrases and clauses often run parallel, as in 'for my part, he keeps me rustically at home, or, to speak more properly, stays me here at home unkept'; or 'unless you could teach me to forget a banished father, you must not learn me how to remember any extraordinary pleasure'. Indeed, some of the longer passages are built up from a series of parallels; examples are 'I have neither the scholar's melancholy, which is emulation; nor the musician's, which is fantastical; nor the courtier's, which is proud . . .' and the paragraphs previously quoted on pages 17 and 23. Such prose is descended from Euphuism or Arcadianism, but it is not Euphuistic, for the balance is never allowed to become mathematical for too long. (If the parallels are piled up momentarily, it is to portray a character's state of mind, and to provide another subject for laughter – as when Rosalind's 'What did he when thou sawest him? What said he? How looked he? Wherein went he? What makes he here? Did he ask for me? Where remains he? How parted he with thee? And when shalt thou see him again? Answer me in one word' earns Celia's mocking reply 'You must borrow me Gargantua's mouth first: 'tis a word too great for any mouth of this age's size. To say "ay" and "no" to these particulars is more than to answer in a catechism.')

Even when the prose is formal in construction, the conversational tone, except in the last scenes, is preserved by such phrases as 'to speak more properly' (in the first sentence quoted in the previous paragraph) or by terms of address: 'Good Monsieur Charles, what's the new news at the new court?' 'There's no news at the court, sir, but the old news.' Celia's 'sweet my coz' or Rosalind's 'O coz, coz, coz, my pretty little coz' are among the many greetings that help similarly to establish the informality; yet because of the tightness of construction (and, of course, the vocabulary) the prose never becomes merely colloquial. Even such a minor point of usage as Shakespeare's choice of 'you' or 'thou' will help to demonstrate the trouble he takes to establish 'tone': the more formal 'you' is used not only by the wrestler Charles to the Duke, by Adam to Orlando, and by Touchstone to Celia but also, originally, by Rosalind (still on her guard, as daughter of the banished Duke) to Celia; 'thou' is used by superior to inferior (the Duke to Charles, Orlando to Adam, and Celia to Touchstone) and, as a mark of affection, by Celia, particularly when trying to put Rosalind at her ease.

The imagery is not obtrusive but is none the less effective for that. It ranges from the flood and the ark, through the English seasons and the Bay of Portugal, to the pearl in the oyster and back to the penalty of Adam; but perhaps the most constant feature, as Caroline Spurgeon noticed many years ago, is the tendency to refer to animals and other aspects of country living: Jaques 'can suck melancholy out of a song, as a weasel sucks eggs'; Rosalind is 'native' to the forest 'as the cony that you see dwell where she is kindled'; Touchstone will be married 'as the ox hath his bow, sir, the horse his curb, and the falcon her bells'; and Rosalind will be more jealous of Orlando 'than a Barbary cock-pigeon over his hen, more clamorous than a parrot against rain, more new-fangled than an ape', and 'more giddy' in her desires 'than a monkey'. This last sentence is followed by a reference to 'Diana in the fountain' that perhaps turned the thoughts of Shakespeare's audience temporarily to the City of London, but the cumulative effect of all the allusions to 'nature' must be to build up the rural 'atmosphere'. As Miss Spurgeon further noted, there is surprisingly little actual description of the forest. The exiled Duke's first speech in Act II, finding tongues in trees, books in the running brooks and sermons in stones, sets the 'scene', but after this the audience must be content with an occasional reference to

an oak whose antick root peeps out
Upon the brook that brawls along this wood

or to sheepcotes, and must rely on its imagination, unconsciously prompted by the imagery, to piece out the 'imperfections' of the bare Elizabethan stage.

One's imagination also has the assistance given by the songs. These – though they are perfect simply as songs and have no greater complexity of language than a song can easily bear – are related even more closely to the themes of the play than, possibly, are the songs in any of Shakespeare's earlier work. 'Under the greenwood tree', for example, helps to establish both the pastoral setting and the tone – and Jaques's third stanza of the song is an important statement of the opposite side of the case; and in much the same way 'What shall he have that killed the deer?' 'enhances the woodland element' but also, with its references to horns and the probability of cuckoldry, maintains the spirit of mocking fun.

Blow, blow, thou winter wind,
Thou art not so unkind
As man's ingratitude,

while still reminding us of 'nature', points up the problem of Adam and Orlando, starving because they are victims of Oliver's 'ingratitude' (nor should one overlook the neat piece of stagecraft that has the song sung at this moment, by Amiens, to give Adam and Orlando time and opportunity to eat). Most magical of all, in the theatre, is the singing by the two Pages of 'It was a lover and his lass' – after Rosalind has arranged the meeting when the couples will be paired off, each lover to his lass as romance decrees. Characteristically, the dramatist introduces the song light-heartedly: 'Shall we clap into't roundly, without hawking, or spitting, or saying we are hoarse, which are the only prologues to a bad voice?' – and again the song has a second theatrical purpose, in that it gives the illusion of the passing of time until the day when Rosalind will present the masque of Hymen.

The wedding masque itself (V.4) is another interesting use of a convention to help round a play off happily (as the Herne the Hunter episode is used to turn *The Merry Wives of Windsor* into a good-humoured joke in which all, even Falstaff, can join). Some commentators have thought that the masque indicates that the Folio text of *As You Like It* represents a revised version performed as part of a wedding celebration, but the hypothesis hardly seems necessary. Elizabethans were accustomed to most forms of 'disguisings', and there are masques in many Elizabethan plays. A masque is a natural and at the same time appropriately formal method of ensuring that

eight . . . must take hands,
To join in Hymen's bands.

The entrance of Jaques de Boys stops the revelling in mid-career, much after the manner of the famous entrance of Mercade to the lovers in *Love's Labour's Lost* with the news that the Princess's father is dead; in *As You Like It*, however, the tidings brought are not chilling but announce the 'conversion' of the usurper and so make possible the completely happy ending, though not without the touch of acid provided by Jaques. Another convention, the epilogue, enables Shakespeare to bring the play to a close, after the stage has been cleared for the boy playing the part of Rosalind; taking advantage both of his true male sex and of his assumed female one, the player appeals to the audience for approval, all but saying to them, in the words of Lodge's address 'To the Gentlemen Readers' of *Rosalynde* that probably gave Shakespeare his title, 'If you like it, so'.

It is difficult to believe that artistry of this order would have been possible even for Shakespeare as early as 1593, the year in which some scholars have placed the composition of the play. There is, to be sure, one passage that may well refer to an important event in that year: Touchstone's 'When a man's verses cannot be understood, nor a man's good wit seconded with the forward child Understanding, it strikes a man more dead than a great reckoning in a little room' (III.3.10–13). Particularly if the last phrase is agreed to be an allusion to Christopher Marlowe's 'infinite riches in a little room' in *The Jew of Malta* (already well-known on the stage, but not published until 1633), there may also be reference to the death of Marlowe in a private room of the inn at Deptford, on 30 May 1593, following a quarrel over a bill or 'reckoning'. It has been suggested, however, by J. H. Walter, that, especially since the preceding lines in *As You Like It* refer to Ovid, Shakespeare may rather have had in mind lines from Chapman's poem *Ovid's Banquet of Sense* (1595): Ovid, seeing Corinna naked, is said to see

> *The fair of beauty, as whole countries come*
> *And show their riches in a little room*

and later Chapman writes that

> *Ovid's muse as in her tropic shined*
> *And he, struck dead, was mere heaven-born become.*

Nor, of course, need a reference to Marlowe's death necessarily have been made immediately after it; Marlowe may have been in Shakespeare's mind following the publication of *Hero and Leander* in 1598. Phebe quotes from that poem:

> *Dead Shepherd, now I find thy saw of might,*
> *'Who ever loved that loved not at first sight?'*

and even though the poem may well have circulated in manuscript, the quotation could hardly have been appreciated by the Elizabethan audience unless the poem had also been published.

Rosalind's words 'I will weep for nothing, like Diana in the fountain' may, but do not necessarily, refer to the fountain with a statue of Diana erected in Cheapside in 1596; Celia's 'since the little wit that fools have was silenced, the little foolery that wise men have makes a great show', in reply to Touchstone's similar sentiments, may, but does not necessarily, refer to a decision of the Privy Council in mid-1599 that Nashe's and Harvey's satirical pamphlets should be burnt and none published thereafter. Jaques's 'seven ages of man' speech may or may not have been prompted by the motto of the new Globe Theatre, probably finished by September 1599. The suggestion, however, that the exiled Duke's opening lines in Act II, in praise of the woodland life, owe something to Robin Hood's words (lines 1365–81) in *The Downfall of Robert Earl of Huntington*, acted in 1598–9, although not conclusive, is tempting (there is no 'source' for these lines in *Rosalynde*); and those who favour an early date for *As You Like It* must also get over the difficulty that it is not included in Meres's list of Shakespeare's well-known plays in 1598 (unless, to be sure, they maintain that *As You Like It*, perhaps in some earlier version, is to be identified with Meres's mysterious *Love's Labour's Won*).

To these possibilities, or probabilities, and the more important evidence of the mature general style of the play, both in verse and in prose, one must add that *As You Like It* was first entered on the Stationers' Register on 4 August 1600; and along with *Henry V* and *Much Ado About Nothing* and Ben Jonson's *Every Man in his Humour* it was entered with the direction 'to be staied' – a phrase almost certainly indicating a move by Shakespeare and his company to prevent 'pirated' or unauthorized publication of a new and popular play. It is surely difficult to reach any other conclusion than that *As You Like It* was written in 1599.

It is still possible, of course, that the play as we have it (it was first published in the First Folio of 1623) was a revision in 1599 of an earlier play – or even that it was revised between 1599 and 1623. There is, however, no good reason for thinking so. Professor Dover Wilson himself later withdrew in great part the theory he had advanced in 1926 that sections of *As You Like It* now in prose must have been originally written in verse. The 'verse-fossils' that he found in the prose – prose that he reduced to verse (sometimes bad verse) by what he called 'a little innocent faking' – could be found by the same method in almost any prose; and, as has been suggested above, when Shakespeare modulates from prose to verse or verse to prose, he generally seems to do so for good dramatic reason. Nor, for that matter, is the verse of *As You Like It* such as even Shakespeare is likely to have been capable of writing in 1593.

The minor inconsistencies that Dover Wilson and others have found in *As You Like It* do exist – or some of them do. But it is not necessary to infer that they betray two stages of composition.

One of them may be of the commentators' own making: for while it is true that Celia says she was 'too young' to value Rosalind when Rosalind's father was banished, this does not necessarily mean that she is thinking of the event as more than, say, a year or eighteen months in the past; a year would be more than long enough for 'old custom' to have made the greenwood life 'more sweet than that of painted pomp'; and while Oliver asks Charles for the 'new news at the new court', Charles gives it to him expressly as 'no news . . . but the old news', of the banishment, and one need assume no more than that Oliver, not living in the new court, has taken a while to catch up with the full details of life there. There is also the convention of 'double time': in many an Elizabethan play time passes more quickly for some purposes of the plot than for others.

Another of the inconsistencies may be removed – and generally has been removed – by a slight textual emendation that seems reasonable enough. In the speech headings of the Folio, the usurping Duke is called simply 'Duke', and his banished brother is 'Duke Senior'; we learn from Orlando in the dialogue, however, at I.2.220–22 that the usurper's name is Frederick, and this is confirmed by Jaques de Boys at V.4.151. Earlier in Act I, scene 2, however, Celia asks Touchstone whom he refers to in his story of the knight who swore by his honour and yet was not forsworn, and Touchstone replies 'One that old Frederick, your father, loves' – to which the Folio allows *Rosalind* to retort: 'My father's love is enough to honour him enough'. Yet it is odd that Touchstone should reply to Celia's question by addressing himself to Rosalind (with 'your father'). 'Old' is not necessarily a reference to age; it was (and still is) a term of half-affectionate familiarity, and Celia would be well entitled to resent a clown's use of it. On the whole, then, it seems more likely that there has been a slip in the speech heading, whether Shakespeare's or the compositor's, and that therefore Celia should be allowed to carry on her exchange with Touchstone, than that Touchstone should turn awkwardly from her to Rosalind and that Shakespeare should thereby name Rosalind's father 'Frederick' as well as Celia's. (Even if the contradiction is permitted to remain, it does not imply that Shakespeare was rewriting the play after a period of time, when he had forgotten the names of his characters: he forgot names during the composition of other plays too.)

The third inconsistency concerns the height of Rosalind and Celia. In Act I, scene 3, Rosalind decides to assume the disguise of the 'man' because she is 'more than common tall', and Celia is content to put herself in mean attire as a girl; and in Act IV, scene 3, Oliver describes 'the boy' (Rosalind) as 'fair', 'the woman' (Celia) as

low
And browner than her brother –

which almost certainly means 'lower and browner' but in any case confirms that Celia is *not* tall. In the source, *Rosalynde*, it is Rosalynde who is the taller; and of course in a whole series of Shakespeare's comedies (including *A Midsummer Night's Dream*, *The Merchant of Venice*, *Much Ado About Nothing*, and *Twelfth Night*) we have one heroine who is tall and fair while the second is short and dark. The problem is that when Orlando in Act I, scene 2, asks Le Beau:

and pray you tell me this,
Which of the two was daughter of the Duke
That here was at the wrestling?

Le Beau replies:

Neither his daughter, if we judge by manners,
But yet indeed the taller is his daughter;
The other is daughter to the banished Duke,
And here detained by her usurping uncle
To keep his daughter company.

This is a plain contradiction, and many editors solve the problem by emending 'taller' to 'smaller' or 'shorter' or 'lesser', thereby setting themselves up as judges of the word that Shakespeare would have used had he said what he is thought to have meant. It seems better to leave the text alone and to assume with Sir Walter Greg and others that for some performance of the play there had been a change of cast, and that the text had been adapted for this at one point and not elsewhere. (Such things still happen in the best organized of playhouses.)

It remains to admit that there are two characters called

Jaques in *As You Like It* – one the confessed cynic, the other the second son of Sir Rowland de Boys, Oliver's and Orlando's brother, who is called Jaques in the first scene and is simply 'Second Brother' in the Folio, when he appears in person in Act V. Quite possibly the two Jaqueses were at first intended to be the one character (the second son in *Rosalynde* is a scholar and a student of philosophy) but if so Shakespeare changed his mind. Again we need not assume that he changed it long after he had forgotten his original plan: a mere duplication of name would hardly have worried the playwright who, not satisfied with all the other complications of *The Taming of the Shrew*, wilfully called one character Gremio and another Grumio.

These are minor matters and do not affect the fact that the Folio text of *As You Like It* is one of the best in the Shakespeare canon. Even if an editor cannot quite, in Sir Arthur Quiller-Couch's optimistic words, 'take holiday', he can certainly 'enjoy his while in Arden'. It is to be hoped that the reader can do so too – and 'fleet the time carelessly' as well.

FURTHER READING

Important editions of *As You Like It* were published in the 1970s. Richard Knowles's New Variorum (1977) gives the reader much material from this and preceding centuries, and Agnes Latham's Arden edition (1975) is acute in its annotation and critical discussion. Superseding these in many ways is Alan Brissenden's impeccably produced Oxford edition (1993), notable for a lengthy and entertaining examination of the history of the play in performance, with an inevitable emphasis on 'famous Rosalinds'.

In the course of Penny Gay's similarly focused book, a lively feminist history of *As You Like It* in the theatre, *As She Likes It: Shakespeare's Unruly Women* (1994), she notes how modern criticism of the play ranges from celebratory variations on festive pastoral to explorations of the dark recesses of the psyche or (even) indictments of a power-hungry urban society. An equally lively and imaginative book by Peter Reynolds in the Penguin Critical Studies Series, '*As You Like It*': *A Dramatic Commentary* (1988), explores this range of interpretation by inventing three directors who describe three very different productions of *As You Like It*: one as an optimistic romance, another as political scandal, and a third as a feminist tract exploring the nature of homosexuality. Drawing a bold moral, Reynolds closes with a stirring injunction to the reader: 'Lay claim to the text on your own behalf, as *you* like it'.

C. L. Barber's seminal work, *Shakespeare's Festive Comedy: A Study of Dramatic Form and its Relation to Social Custom* (1959), is probably the most famous instance of the case for festive celebration. Arden isn't Jonson's

London, he reminds us. Similarly, John Russell Brown in *Shakespeare and His Comedies* (1962) finds much in the play to celebrate, especially the 'peculiar delightfulness' of love's order. 'A heaven-sent euphoria' is Ruth Nevo's description of Arden in *Comic Transformations in Shakespeare* (1980). And R. C. Hassel's biblically minded *Faith and Folly in Shakespeare's Romantic Comedies* (1980) expands the notion of celebration to emphasize the educative value of the games the lovers play. E. J. Jensen's *Shakespeare and the Ends of Comedy* (1991) urges us to value these games without bothering too much about how the plays end (with the return to the patriarchal status quo), despite the arguments to the contrary by a host of critics, including C. L. Barber and Northrop Frye. Hassel urges us to abandon our traditional concern for 'teleological design' – there is no isolable truth, he says, enacted in the final scene – and also to eschew distorted interpretations of the play like Jan Kott's 'bitter Arcadia'. Robert Ornstein in *Shakespeare's Comedies: From Roman Farce to Romantic Mystery* (1986) also takes issue with Frye and Barber – a different issue, though – in his convincing argument that *As You Like It* is romantic rather than festive, informed by a feminine rather than a masculine sensibility. His conclusion seems unimpeachable: 'Rosalind and Touchstone are whimsical, yea-saying sceptics who affirm the values they seem to mock'.

The bitterness of Arcadia is a concern, however. G. Beiner's *Shakespeare's Agonistic Comedy: Poetics, Analysis, Criticism* (1933), for instance, argues that the function of Rosalind/Ganymede is, like Portia's in *The Merchant of Venice*, to enact a comic exorcism of the fear of adultery. W. Thomas MacCary's *Friends and Lovers: the Phenomenology of Desire in Shakespearean Comedy* (1985) maintains that the pattern of desire in Shakespeare's romantic comedies is narcissistic. He makes claims for the comedies that would have raised an eyebrow in the earlier part of the century: they are 'comparable in profundity, complexity, and completeness to the dialogues of Plato and the metapsychological essays of Freud'. His enthusiasm is matched by J. P. Ward in his Harvester New Critical Introduction to *As You Like It* (1992), which he describes as 'a play of the most extraordinarily elusive subtlety'. (This is one of the weaker books in this uneven series.) Valerie Traub's *Desire and Anxiety: Circulations of Sexuality in Shakespearean Drama* (1992) argues that the 'specifically erotic valence' of transvestism in *As You Like It* enables the exploration of homoeroticism. Dark recesses, indeed! A similar uneasiness about the relations between the sexes in the play informs Marianne Novy's *Gender Relations in Shakespeare* (1984) and Marilyn L. Williamson's *The Patriarchy of Shakespeare's Comedies* (1986), which, like Peter Erickson's *Patriarchal Structures in Shakespeare's Drama* (1985), explores the dark recess of the tyranny of the male in *As You Like It*. For Erickson, the restoration of that tyranny at the play's close is underscored by the revelation in the Epilogue by Rosalind that she is a boy. (A robustly Rabelaisian counterview can be found in Juliet Dusinberre's 'As *Who* Liked It?' in *Shakespeare Survey 46* (1994), where the *who* in the title's question were the women in the audience, egged on by a high-spirited Rosalind. No boy she, as far as Dusinberre is concerned.)

More conventional, usefully introductory studies of *As You Like It* include: Ralph Berry's *Shakespeare's Comedies: Explorations in Form* (1972), Kenneth Muir's *Shakespeare's Comic Sequence* (1979), Bertrand Evans's *Shakespeare's Comedies* (1960), Michael Jamieson's *Shakespeare: 'As You Like It', Studies in English Literature 25* (1965) (an act-by-act commentary), Leo Salingar's *Shakespeare and the Traditions of Comedy* (1974), Alexander Leggatt's *Shakespeare's Comedy of Love* (1974) (valuable for its thoughtful analysis of the *differences* between the romantic comedies – compare Berry), Anthony J. Lewis's *Love Story in Shakespearean Comedy* (1992), Ronald C. Macdonald's *William Shakespeare: The Comedies* (1992), Peter G. Phialas's *Shake-*

speare's Romantic Comedies: the Development of their Form and Meaning (1966) (self-confessedly introductory), and David Richman's *Laughter, Pain, and Wonder: Shakespeare's Comedies and the Audience in the Theater* (1990). John Russell Brown's selection of essays on *Much Ado* and *As You Like It* in the Casebook Series (1979) is to be commended for its section on the comedies on the stage and for reprinting Sherman Hawkins's invaluable essay 'The Two Worlds of Shakespearean Comedy'.

Michael Taylor, 1995

AS YOU LIKE IT

THE CHARACTERS IN THE PLAY

DUKE SENIOR, a banished duke

AMIENS }
JAQUES } noblemen in attendance on him

DUKE FREDERICK, his brother, the usurper

LE BEAU, a courtier

CHARLES, a wrestler

OLIVER }
JAQUES } sons of Sir Rowland de Boys
ORLANDO }

ADAM }
DENNIS } servants of Oliver

THE CLOWN, alias TOUCHSTONE

SIR OLIVER MARTEXT, a country vicar

CORIN }
SILVIUS } shepherds

WILLIAM, a country youth, in love with Audrey

ROSALIND, daughter of Duke Senior, later disguised as GANYMEDE

CELIA, daughter of Duke Frederick, later disguised as ALIENA

PHEBE, a shepherdess

AUDREY, a country wench

A masquer representing HYMEN

Lords, pages, and attendants

Enter Orlando and Adam I.1

ORLANDO As I remember, Adam, it was upon this fashion bequeathed me by will, but poor a thousand crowns, and, as thou sayest, charged my brother on his blessing to breed me well; and there begins my sadness. My brother Jaques he keeps at school, and report speaks goldenly of his profit: for my part, he keeps me rustically at home, or, to speak more properly, stays me here at home unkept – for call you that 'keeping' for a gentleman of my birth, that differs not from the stalling of an ox? His horses are bred better, for, besides that they 10 are fair with their feeding, they are taught their manage, and to that end riders dearly hired; but I, his brother, gain nothing under him but growth, for the which his animals on his dunghills are as much bound to him as I. Besides this nothing that he so plentifully gives me, the something that nature gave me his countenance seems to take from me: he lets me feed with his hinds, bars me the place of a brother, and, as much as in him lies, mines my gentility with my education. This is it, Adam, that grieves me, and the spirit of my father, which I think is 20 within me, begins to mutiny against this servitude. I will no longer endure it, though yet I know no wise remedy how to avoid it.

Enter Oliver

ADAM Yonder comes my master, your brother.

ORLANDO Go apart, Adam, and thou shalt hear how he will shake me up.

Adam stands aside

OLIVER Now, sir, what make you here?

ORLANDO Nothing: I am not taught to make anything.

OLIVER What mar you then, sir?

30 ORLANDO Marry, sir, I am helping you to mar that which God made, a poor unworthy brother of yours, with idleness.

OLIVER Marry, sir, be better employed, and be naught a while.

ORLANDO Shall I keep your hogs and eat husks with them? What prodigal portion have I spent, that I should come to such penury?

OLIVER Know you where you are, sir?

ORLANDO O, sir, very well: here in your orchard.

40 OLIVER Know you before whom, sir?

ORLANDO Ay, better than him I am before knows me: I know you are my eldest brother, and in the gentle condition of blood you should so know me. The courtesy of nations allows you my better, in that you are the first born, but the same tradition takes not away my blood, were there twenty brothers betwixt us: I have as much of my father in me as you, albeit I confess your coming before me is nearer to his reverence.

OLIVER (*threatening him*) What, boy!

50 ORLANDO (*seizing him by the throat*) Come, come, elder brother, you are too young in this.

OLIVER Wilt thou lay hands on me, villain?

ORLANDO I am no villain: I am the youngest son of Sir Rowland de Boys; he was my father, and he is thrice a villain that says such a father begot villains. Wert thou not my brother, I would not take this hand from thy throat till this other had pulled out thy tongue for saying so; thou hast railed on thyself.

ADAM (*coming forward*) Sweet masters, be patient; for

your father's remembrance, be at accord. 60

OLIVER Let me go, I say.

ORLANDO I will not till I please: you shall hear me. My father charged you in his will to give me good education: you have trained me like a peasant, obscuring and hiding from me all gentleman-like qualities. The spirit of my father grows strong in me, and I will no longer endure it. Therefore allow me such exercises as may become a gentleman, or give me the poor allottery my father left me by testament; with that I will go buy my fortunes.

OLIVER And what wilt thou do, beg when that is spent? 70 Well, sir, get you in. I will not long be troubled with you: you shall have some part of your will. I pray you, leave me.

ORLANDO I will no further offend you than becomes me for my good.

OLIVER Get you with him, you old dog.

ADAM Is 'old dog' my reward? Most true, I have lost my teeth in your service. God be with my old master! He would not have spoke such a word.

Exeunt Orlando and Adam

OLIVER Is it even so? Begin you to grow upon me? I will 80 physic your rankness, and yet give no thousand crowns neither. Holla, Dennis!

Enter Dennis

DENNIS Calls your worship?

OLIVER Was not Charles, the Duke's wrestler, here to speak with me?

DENNIS So please you, he is here at the door, and importunes access to you.

OLIVER Call him in. *Exit Dennis*

'Twill be a good way – and tomorrow the wrestling is.

Enter Charles

CHARLES Good morrow to your worship. 90

OLIVER Good Monsieur Charles, what's the new news at the new court?

CHARLES There's no news at the court, sir, but the old news: that is, the old Duke is banished by his younger brother the new Duke, and three or four loving lords have put themselves into voluntary exile with him, whose lands and revenues enrich the new Duke; therefore he gives them good leave to wander.

OLIVER Can you tell if Rosalind, the Duke's daughter, be
100 banished with her father?

CHARLES O, no; for the Duke's daughter, her cousin, so loves her, being ever from their cradles bred together, that she would have followed her exile, or have died to stay behind her; she is at the court, and no less beloved of her uncle than his own daughter, and never two ladies loved as they do.

OLIVER Where will the old Duke live?

CHARLES They say he is already in the Forest of Arden, and a many merry men with him; and there they live
110 like the old Robin Hood of England: they say many young gentlemen flock to him every day, and fleet the time carelessly as they did in the golden world.

OLIVER What, you wrestle tomorrow before the new Duke?

CHARLES Marry do I, sir; and I came to acquaint you with a matter. I am given, sir, secretly to understand that your younger brother, Orlando, hath a disposition to come in disguised against me to try a fall. Tomorrow, sir, I wrestle for my credit, and he that escapes me
120 without some broken limb shall acquit him well. Your brother is but young and tender, and for your love I would be loath to foil him, as I must for my own honour if he come in. Therefore, out of my love to you, I came hither to acquaint you withal, that either you might

stay him from his intendment, or brook such disgrace well as he shall run into, in that it is a thing of his own search, and altogether against my will.

OLIVER Charles, I thank thee for thy love to me, which thou shalt find I will most kindly requite. I had myself notice of my brother's purpose herein, and have by underhand means laboured to dissuade him from it; but he is resolute. I'll tell thee, Charles, it is the stubbornest young fellow of France, full of ambition, an envious emulator of every man's good parts, a secret and villainous contriver against me, his natural brother. Therefore use thy discretion; I had as lief thou didst break his neck as his finger. And thou wert best look to't; for if thou dost him any slight disgrace, or if he do not mightily grace himself on thee, he will practise against thee by poison, entrap thee by some treacherous device, and never leave thee till he hath ta'en thy life by some indirect means or other: for, I assure thee – and almost with tears I speak it – there is not one so young and so villainous this day living. I speak but brotherly of him, but should I anatomize him to thee as he is, I must blush and weep, and thou must look pale and wonder.

130

140

CHARLES I am heartily glad I came hither to you. If he come tomorrow, I'll give him his payment: if ever he go alone again, I'll never wrestle for prize more. And so God keep your worship! *Exit*

150

OLIVER Farewell, good Charles. Now will I stir this gamester. I hope I shall see an end of him, for my soul – yet I know not why – hates nothing more than he. Yet he's gentle, never schooled and yet learned, full of noble device, of all sorts enchantingly beloved, and indeed so much in the heart of the world, and especially of my own people, who best know him, that I am

altogether misprized. But it shall not be so long; this
160 wrestler shall clear all. Nothing remains but that I
kindle the boy thither, which now I'll go about. *Exit*

I.2 *Enter Rosalind and Celia*

CELIA I pray thee, Rosalind, sweet my coz, be merry.

ROSALIND Dear Celia, I show more mirth than I am mistress of, and would you yet were merrier. Unless you could teach me to forget a banished father, you must not learn me how to remember any extraordinary pleasure.

CELIA Herein I see thou lovest me not with the full weight that I love thee. If my uncle, thy banished father, had banished thy uncle, the Duke my father, so thou hadst
10 been still with me, I could have taught my love to take thy father for mine; so wouldst thou, if the truth of thy love to me were so righteously tempered as mine is to thee.

ROSALIND Well, I will forget the condition of my estate, to rejoice in yours.

CELIA You know my father hath no child but I, nor none is like to have; and truly, when he dies, thou shalt be his heir: for what he hath taken away from thy father perforce, I will render thee again in affection, by mine
20 honour I will, and when I break that oath, let me turn monster. Therefore, my sweet Rose, my dear Rose, be merry.

ROSALIND From henceforth I will, coz, and devise sports. Let me see – what think you of falling in love?

CELIA Marry, I prithee do, to make sport withal; but love no man in good earnest, nor no further in sport neither, than with safety of a pure blush thou mayst in honour come off again.

ROSALIND What shall be our sport then?

CELIA Let us sit and mock the good housewife Fortune 30
from her wheel, that her gifts may henceforth be bestowed equally.

ROSALIND I would we could do so; for her benefits are mightily misplaced, and the bountiful blind woman doth most mistake in her gifts to women.

CELIA 'Tis true, for those that she makes fair she scarce makes honest, and those that she makes honest she makes very ill-favouredly.

ROSALIND Nay, now thou goest from Fortune's office to Nature's: Fortune reigns in gifts of the world, not in 40
the lineaments of Nature.

Enter Touchstone

CELIA No; when Nature hath made a fair creature, may she not by Fortune fall into the fire? Though Nature hath given us wit to flout at Fortune, hath not Fortune sent in this fool to cut off the argument?

ROSALIND Indeed, there is Fortune too hard for Nature, when Fortune makes Nature's natural the cutter-off of Nature's wit.

CELIA Peradventure this is not Fortune's work neither, but Nature's, who perceiveth our natural wits too dull 50
to reason of such goddesses and hath sent this natural for our whetstone: for always the dullness of the fool is the whetstone of the wits. How now, wit, whither wander you?

TOUCHSTONE Mistress, you must come away to your father.

CELIA Were you made the messenger?

TOUCHSTONE No, by mine honour, but I was bid to come for you.

ROSALIND Where learned you that oath, fool? 60

TOUCHSTONE Of a certain knight that swore by his

honour they were good pancakes and swore by his honour the mustard was naught: now I'll stand to it the pancakes were naught and the mustard was good, and yet was not the knight forsworn.

CELIA How prove you that, in the great heap of your knowledge?

ROSALIND Ay, marry, now unmuzzle your wisdom.

TOUCHSTONE Stand you both forth now: stroke your
70 chins and swear by your beards that I am a knave.

CELIA By our beards – if we had them – thou art.

TOUCHSTONE By my knavery – if I had it – then I were; but if you swear by that that is not, you are not forsworn: no more was this knight, swearing by his honour, for he never had any; or if he had, he had sworn it away before ever he saw those pancakes or that mustard.

CELIA Prithee, who is't that thou meanest?

TOUCHSTONE One that old Frederick, your father, loves.

CELIA My father's love is enough to honour him enough.
80 Speak no more of him; you'll be whipped for taxation one of these days.

TOUCHSTONE The more pity that fools may not speak wisely what wise men do foolishly.

CELIA By my troth, thou sayest true: for since the little wit that fools have was silenced, the little foolery that wise men have makes a great show. Here comes Monsieur the Beu.

Enter Le Beau

ROSALIND With his mouth full of news.

CELIA Which he will put on us, as pigeons feed their
90 young.

ROSALIND Then shall we be news-crammed.

CELIA All the better: we shall be the more marketable. *Bon jour*, Monsieur Le Beau, what's the news?

LE BEAU Fair princess, you have lost much good sport.

CELIA Sport? Of what colour?

LE BEAU What colour, madam? How shall I answer you?
ROSALIND As wit and fortune will.
TOUCHSTONE Or as the Destinies decrees.
CELIA Well said, that was laid on with a trowel.
TOUCHSTONE Nay, if I keep not my rank – 100
ROSALIND Thou losest thy old smell.
LE BEAU You amaze me, ladies. I would have told you of good wrestling, which you have lost the sight of.
ROSALIND Yet tell us the manner of the wrestling.
LE BEAU I will tell you the beginning; and, if it please your ladyships, you may see the end, for the best is yet to do, and here, where you are, they are coming to perform it.
CELIA Well, the beginning that is dead and buried.
LE BEAU There comes an old man and his three sons – 110
CELIA I could match this beginning with an old tale.
LE BEAU Three proper young men, of excellent growth and presence –
ROSALIND With bills on their necks: 'Be it known unto all men by these presents'.
LE BEAU The eldest of the three wrestled with Charles, the Duke's wrestler, which Charles in a moment threw him, and broke three of his ribs, that there is little hope of life in him. So he served the second, and so the third. Yonder they lie, the poor old man their father making 120 such pitiful dole over them that all the beholders take his part with weeping.
ROSALIND Alas!
TOUCHSTONE But what is the sport, Monsieur, that the ladies have lost?
LE BEAU Why, this that I speak of.
TOUCHSTONE Thus men may grow wiser every day. It is the first time that ever I heard breaking of ribs was sport for ladies.
CELIA Or I, I promise thee. 130

ROSALIND But is there any else longs to see this broken music in his sides? Is there yet another dotes upon rib-breaking? Shall we see this wrestling, cousin?

LE BEAU You must if you stay here, for here is the place appointed for the wrestling, and they are ready to perform it.

CELIA Yonder, sure, they are coming. Let us now stay and see it.

Flourish. Enter Duke Frederick, Lords, Orlando, Charles, and attendants

DUKE Come on. Since the youth will not be entreated, his
140 own peril on his forwardness.

ROSALIND Is yonder the man?

LE BEAU Even he, madam.

CELIA Alas, he is too young; yet he looks successfully.

DUKE How now, daughter and cousin? Are you crept hither to see the wrestling?

ROSALIND Ay, my liege, so please you give us leave.

DUKE You will take little delight in it, I can tell you, there is such odds in the man. In pity of the challenger's youth I would fain dissuade him, but he will not be
150 entreated. Speak to him, ladies, see if you can move him.

CELIA Call him hither, good Monsieur Le Beau.

DUKE Do so: I'll not be by.

He stands aside

LE BEAU Monsieur the challenger, the princess calls for you.

ORLANDO I attend them with all respect and duty.

ROSALIND Young man, have you challenged Charles the wrestler?

ORLANDO No, fair Princess. He is the general challenger; I come but in as others do, to try with him the strength
160 of my youth.

CELIA Young gentleman, your spirits are too bold for your years. You have seen cruel proof of this man's strength; if you saw yourself with your eyes, or knew yourself with your judgement, the fear of your adventure would counsel you to a more equal enterprise. We pray you for your own sake to embrace your own safety, and give over this attempt.

ROSALIND Do, young sir, your reputation shall not therefore be misprized: we will make it our suit to the Duke that the wrestling might not go forward. 170

ORLANDO I beseech you, punish me not with your hard thoughts, wherein I confess me much guilty to deny so fair and excellent ladies anything. But let your fair eyes and gentle wishes go with me to my trial: wherein if I be foiled, there is but one shamed that was never gracious; if killed, but one dead that is willing to be so. I shall do my friends no wrong, for I have none to lament me; the world no injury, for in it I have nothing: only in the world I fill up a place which may be better supplied when I have made it empty. 180

ROSALIND The little strength that I have, I would it were with you.

CELIA And mine, to eke out hers.

ROSALIND Fare you well. Pray heaven, I be deceived in you!

CELIA Your heart's desires be with you!

CHARLES Come, where is this young gallant that is so desirous to lie with his mother earth?

ORLANDO Ready, sir, but his will hath in it a more modest working. 190

DUKE You shall try but one fall.

CHARLES No, I warrant your grace, you shall not entreat him to a second, that have so mightily persuaded him from a first.

ORLANDO You mean to mock me after; you should not have mocked me before. But come your ways!

ROSALIND Now Hercules be thy speed, young man!

CELIA I would I were invisible, to catch the strong fellow by the leg.

Orlando and Charles wrestle

200 ROSALIND O excellent young man!

CELIA If I had a thunderbolt in mine eye, I can tell who should down.

A shout as Charles is thrown

DUKE (*coming forward*) No more, no more.

ORLANDO Yes, I beseech your grace, I am not yet well breathed.

DUKE How dost thou, Charles?

LE BEAU He cannot speak, my lord.

DUKE Bear him away.

Attendants carry Charles off

What is thy name, young man?

210 ORLANDO Orlando, my liege; the youngest son of Sir Rowland de Boys.

DUKE

I would thou hadst been son to some man else.
The world esteemed thy father honourable,
But I did find him still mine enemy.
Thou shouldst have better pleased me with this deed
Hadst thou descended from another house.
But fare thee well, thou art a gallant youth;
I would thou hadst told me of another father.

Exit Duke, with Lords, Le Beau, and Touchstone

CELIA

Were I my father, coz, would I do this?

ORLANDO

220 I am more proud to be Sir Rowland's son,
His youngest son, and would not change that calling
To be adopted heir to Frederick.

ROSALIND

My father loved Sir Rowland as his soul,

And all the world was of my father's mind.
Had I before known this young man his son,
I should have given him tears unto entreaties
Ere he should thus have ventured.

CELIA Gentle cousin,
Let us go thank him, and encourage him.
My father's rough and envious disposition
Sticks me at heart. – Sir, you have well deserved. 230
If you do keep your promises in love
But justly as you have exceeded all promise,
Your mistress shall be happy.

ROSALIND (*taking a chain from her neck*)
Gentleman,
Wear this for me – one out of suits with fortune,
That could give more but that her hand lacks means.
(*to Celia*) Shall we go, coz?

CELIA Ay. Fare you well, fair gentleman.

Rosalind and Celia begin to withdraw

ORLANDO
Can I not say 'I thank you'? My better parts
Are all thrown down, and that which here stands up
Is but a quintain, a mere lifeless block. 240

ROSALIND
He calls us back. My pride fell with my fortunes:
I'll ask him what he would. – Did you call, sir?
Sir, you have wrestled well, and overthrown
More than your enemies.

CELIA Will you go, coz?

ROSALIND
Have with you. (*To Orlando*) Fare you well.

Exeunt Rosalind and Celia

ORLANDO
What passion hangs these weights upon my tongue?
I cannot speak to her, yet she urged conference.

Enter Le Beau

O poor Orlando, thou art overthrown!
Or Charles or something weaker masters thee.

LE BEAU

250 Good sir, I do in friendship counsel you
To leave this place. Albeit you have deserved
High commendation, true applause, and love,
Yet such is now the Duke's condition,
That he misconsters all that you have done.
The Duke is humorous – what he is, indeed,
More suits you to conceive than I to speak of.

ORLANDO

I thank you, sir; and pray you tell me this,
Which of the two was daughter of the Duke
That here was at the wrestling?

LE BEAU

260 Neither his daughter, if we judge by manners,
But yet indeed the taller is his daughter;
The other is daughter to the banished Duke,
And here detained by her usurping uncle
To keep his daughter company, whose loves
Are dearer than the natural bond of sisters.
But I can tell you that of late this Duke
Hath ta'en displeasure 'gainst his gentle niece,
Grounded upon no other argument
But that the people praise her for her virtues
270 And pity her for her good father's sake;
And, on my life, his malice 'gainst the lady
Will suddenly break forth. Sir, fare you well;
Hereafter, in a better world than this,
I shall desire more love and knowledge of you.

ORLANDO

I rest much bounden to you: fare you well.

Exit Le Beau

Thus must I from the smoke into the smother,
From tyrant Duke unto a tyrant brother.
But heavenly Rosalind! *Exit*

Enter Celia and Rosalind I.3

CELIA Why cousin, why Rosalind, Cupid have mercy, not a word?

ROSALIND Not one to throw at a dog.

CELIA No, thy words are too precious to be cast away upon curs; throw some of them at me. Come, lame me with reasons.

ROSALIND Then there were two cousins laid up, when the one should be lamed with reasons, and the other mad without any.

CELIA But is all this for your father? 10

ROSALIND No, some of it is for my child's father. – O, how full of briars is this working-day world!

CELIA They are but burs, cousin, thrown upon thee in holiday foolery. If we walk not in the trodden paths, our very petticoats will catch them.

ROSALIND I could shake them off my coat; these burs are in my heart.

CELIA Hem them away.

ROSALIND I would try, if I could cry 'hem' and have him. 20

CELIA Come, come, wrestle with thy affections.

ROSALIND O, they take the part of a better wrestler than myself.

CELIA O, a good wish upon you; you will try in time, in despite of a fall. But turning these jests out of service, let us talk in good earnest: is it possible on such a sudden you should fall into so strong a liking with old Sir Rowland's youngest son?

ROSALIND The Duke my father loved his father dearly.

30 CELIA Doth it therefore ensue that you should love his son dearly? By this kind of chase, I should hate him, for my father hated his father dearly; yet I hate not Orlando.

ROSALIND No, faith, hate him not, for my sake.

CELIA Why should I not? Doth he not deserve well?

Enter Duke, with Lords

ROSALIND Let me love him for that, and do you love him because I do. – Look, here comes the Duke.

CELIA With his eyes full of anger.

DUKE
Mistress, dispatch you with your safest haste
And get you from our court.

ROSALIND Me, uncle?

40 DUKE You, cousin.
Within these ten days if that thou beest found
So near our public court as twenty miles,
Thou diest for it.

ROSALIND I do beseech your grace,
Let me the knowledge of my fault bear with me.
If with myself I hold intelligence
Or have acquaintance with mine own desires,
If that I do not dream or be not frantic –
As I do trust I am not – then, dear uncle,
Never so much as in a thought unborn
Did I offend your highness.

50 DUKE Thus do all traitors:
If their purgation did consist in words,
They are as innocent as grace itself.
Let it suffice thee that I trust thee not.

ROSALIND
Yet your mistrust cannot make me a traitor.
Tell me whereon the likelihoods depends.

DUKE
Thou art thy father's daughter, there's enough.
ROSALIND
So was I when your highness took his dukedom,
So was I when your highness banished him.
Treason is not inherited, my lord,
Or, if we did derive it from our friends, 60
What's that to me? My father was no traitor;
Then, good my liege, mistake me not so much
To think my poverty is treacherous.
CELIA
Dear sovereign, hear me speak.
DUKE
Ay, Celia, we stayed her for your sake,
Else had she with her father ranged along.
CELIA
I did not then entreat to have her stay;
It was your pleasure and your own remorse.
I was too young that time to value her,
But now I know her. If she be a traitor, 70
Why so am I: we still have slept together,
Rose at an instant, learned, played, eat together,
And wheresoe'er we went, like Juno's swans
Still we went coupled and inseparable.
DUKE
She is too subtle for thee, and her smoothness,
Her very silence, and her patience
Speak to the people, and they pity her.
Thou art a fool; she robs thee of thy name,
And thou wilt show more bright and seem more virtuous
When she is gone. Then open not thy lips: 80
Firm and irrevocable is my doom
Which I have passed upon her; she is banished.

CELIA

Pronounce that sentence then on me, my liege,
I cannot live out of her company.

DUKE

You are a fool. – You, niece, provide yourself.
If you outstay the time, upon mine honour
And in the greatness of my word, you die.

Exit Duke, with Lords

CELIA

O my poor Rosalind, whither wilt thou go?
Wilt thou change fathers? I will give thee mine.
90 I charge thee, be not thou more grieved than I am.

ROSALIND

I have more cause.

CELIA Thou hast not, cousin.
Prithee, be cheerful; knowest thou not the Duke
Hath banished me, his daughter?

ROSALIND That he hath not.

CELIA

No, hath not? Rosalind lacks then the love
Which teacheth thee that thou and I am one.
Shall we be sundered? Shall we part, sweet girl?
No, let my father seek another heir.
Therefore devise with me how we may fly,
Whither to go, and what to bear with us,
100 And do not seek to take your change upon you,
To bear your griefs yourself and leave me out;
For, by this heaven, now at our sorrows pale,
Say what thou canst, I'll go along with thee.

ROSALIND

Why, whither shall we go?

CELIA

To seek my uncle in the Forest of Arden.

ROSALIND

Alas, what danger will it be to us,

Maids as we are, to travel forth so far?
Beauty provoketh thieves sooner than gold.

CELIA
I'll put myself in poor and mean attire
And with a kind of umber smirch my face. 110
The like do you; so shall we pass along
And never stir assailants.

ROSALIND Were it not better,
Because that I am more than common tall,
That I did suit me all points like a man?
A gallant curtle-axe upon my thigh,
A boar-spear in my hand, and in my heart
Lie there what hidden woman's fear there will,
We'll have a swashing and a martial outside,
As many other mannish cowards have
That do outface it with their semblances. 120

CELIA
What shall I call thee when thou art a man?

ROSALIND
I'll have no worse a name than Jove's own page,
And therefore look you call me 'Ganymede'.
But what will you be called?

CELIA
Something that hath a reference to my state:
No longer 'Celia', but 'Aliena'.

ROSALIND
But, cousin, what if we assayed to steal
The clownish fool out of your father's court:
Would he not be a comfort to our travel?

CELIA
He'll go along o'er the wide world with me. 130
Leave me alone to woo him. Let's away
And get our jewels and our wealth together,
Devise the fittest time and safest way
To hide us from pursuit that will be made

After my flight. Now go in we content
To liberty, and not to banishment. *Exeunt*

*

II.1 *Enter Duke Senior, Amiens, and two or three Lords dressed like foresters*

DUKE

Now my co-mates and brothers in exile,
Hath not old custom made this life more sweet
Than that of painted pomp? Are not these woods
More free from peril than the envious court?
Here feel we not the penalty of Adam,
The seasons' difference, as the icy fang
And churlish chiding of the winter's wind,
Which when it bites and blows upon my body
Even till I shrink with cold, I smile and say
10 'This is no flattery; these are counsellors
That feelingly persuade me what I am'?
Sweet are the uses of adversity,
Which, like the toad, ugly and venomous,
Wears yet a precious jewel in his head;
And this our life, exempt from public haunt,
Finds tongues in trees, books in the running brooks,
Sermons in stones, and good in everything.

AMIENS

I would not change it. Happy is your grace
That can translate the stubbornness of fortune
20 Into so quiet and so sweet a style.

DUKE

Come, shall we go and kill us venison?
And yet it irks me the poor dappled fools,
Being native burghers of this desert city,

Should in their own confines with forkèd heads
Have their round haunches gored.

FIRST LORD Indeed, my lord,
The melancholy Jaques grieves at that
And, in that kind, swears you do more usurp
Than doth your brother that hath banished you.
Today my lord of Amiens and myself
Did steal behind him as he lay along 30
Under an oak whose antick root peeps out
Upon the brook that brawls along this wood,
To the which place a poor sequestered stag
That from the hunter's aim had ta'en a hurt
Did come to languish; and indeed, my lord,
The wretched animal heaved forth such groans
That their discharge did stretch his leathern coat
Almost to bursting, and the big round tears
Coursed one another down his innocent nose
In piteous chase; and thus the hairy fool, 40
Much markèd of the melancholy Jaques,
Stood on th'extremest verge of the swift brook
Augmenting it with tears.

DUKE But what said Jaques?
Did he not moralize this spectacle?

FIRST LORD
O, yes, into a thousand similes.
First, for his weeping into the needless stream:
'Poor deer,' quoth he, 'thou makest a testament
As worldlings do, giving thy sum of more
To that which had too much.' Then, being there
alone,
Left and abandoned of his velvet friend, 50
' 'Tis right,' quoth he, 'thus misery doth part
The flux of company.' Anon a careless herd,
Full of the pasture, jumps along by him

And never stays to greet him: 'Ay,' quoth Jaques,
'Sweep on, you fat and greasy citizens,
'Tis just the fashion! Wherefore do you look
Upon that poor and broken bankrupt there?'
Thus most invectively he pierceth through
The body of country, city, court,
60 Yea, and of this our life, swearing that we
Are mere usurpers, tyrants, and what's worse
To fright the animals and to kill them up
In their assigned and native dwelling place.

DUKE
And did you leave him in this contemplation?

SECOND LORD
We did, my lord, weeping and commenting
Upon the sobbing deer.

DUKE Show me the place;
I love to cope him in these sullen fits,
For then he's full of matter.

FIRST LORD
I'll bring you to him straight. *Exeunt*

II.2 *Enter Duke Frederick, with Lords*

DUKE
Can it be possible that no man saw them?
It cannot be; some villains of my court
Are of consent and sufferance in this.

FIRST LORD
I cannot hear of any that did see her.
The ladies her attendants of her chamber
Saw her abed, and in the morning early
They found the bed untreasured of their mistress.

SECOND LORD
My lord, the roynish clown at whom so oft

Your grace was wont to laugh is also missing.
Hisperia, the princess' gentlewoman, 10
Confesses that she secretly o'erheard
Your daughter and her cousin much commend
The parts and graces of the wrestler
That did but lately foil the sinewy Charles,
And she believes wherever they are gone
That youth is surely in their company.

DUKE

Send to his brother; fetch that gallant hither.
If he be absent, bring his brother to me;
I'll make him find him. Do this suddenly,
And let not search and inquisition quail 20
To bring again these foolish runaways.

Exeunt

Enter Orlando and Adam from opposite sides II.3

ORLANDO Who's there?

ADAM

What, my young master? O my gentle master,
O my sweet master, O you memory
Of old Sir Rowland, why, what make you here?
Why are you virtuous? Why do people love you?
And wherefore are you gentle, strong, and valiant?
Why would you be so fond to overcome
The bonny prizer of the humorous Duke?
Your praise is come too swiftly home before you.
Know you not, master, to some kind of men 10
Their graces serve them but as enemies?
No more do yours; your virtues, gentle master,
Are sanctified and holy traitors to you.
O, what a world is this, when what is comely
Envenoms him that bears it!

ORLANDO

Why, what's the matter?

ADAM O unhappy youth,

Come not within these doors; within this roof
The enemy of all your graces lives.
Your brother – no, no brother – yet the son –
20 Yet not the son, I will not call him son
Of him I was about to call his father –
Hath heard your praises, and this night he means
To burn the lodging where you use to lie,
And you within it. If he fail of that,
He will have other means to cut you off.
I overheard him, and his practices.
This is no place, this house is but a butchery;
Abhor it, fear it, do not enter it.

ORLANDO

Why, whither, Adam, wouldst thou have me go?

ADAM

30 No matter whither, so you come not here.

ORLANDO

What, wouldst thou have me go and beg my food,
Or with a base and boisterous sword enforce
A thievish living on the common road?
This I must do, or know not what to do:
Yet this I will not do, do how I can.
I rather will subject me to the malice
Of a diverted blood and bloody brother.

ADAM

But do not so. I have five hundred crowns,
The thrifty hire I saved under your father,
40 Which I did store to be my foster-nurse
When service should in my old limbs lie lame
And unregarded age in corners thrown.
Take that, and He that doth the ravens feed,
Yea, providently caters for the sparrow,

Be comfort to my age. Here is the gold;
All this I give you. Let me be your servant.
Though I look old, yet I am strong and lusty,
For in my youth I never did apply
Hot and rebellious liquors in my blood,
Nor did not with unbashful forehead woo 50
The means of weakness and debility;
Therefore my age is as a lusty winter,
Frosty, but kindly. Let me go with you,
I'll do the service of a younger man
In all your business and necessities.

ORLANDO

O good old man, how well in thee appears
The constant service of the antique world,
When service sweat for duty, not for meed!
Thou art not for the fashion of these times,
Where none will sweat but for promotion, 60
And having that do choke their service up
Even with the having; it is not so with thee.
But, poor old man, thou prunest a rotten tree
That cannot so much as a blossom yield
In lieu of all thy pains and husbandry.
But come thy ways, we'll go along together,
And ere we have thy youthful wages spent
We'll light upon some settled low content.

ADAM

Master, go on, and I will follow thee
To the last gasp with truth and loyalty. 70
From seventeen years till now almost fourscore
Here lived I, but now live here no more.
At seventeen years many their fortunes seek,
But at fourscore it is too late a week.
Yet fortune cannot recompense me better
Than to die well, and not my master's debtor. *Exeunt*

II.4 *Enter Rosalind as Ganymede, Celia as Aliena, and the Clown, alias Touchstone*

ROSALIND O Jupiter, how weary are my spirits!

TOUCHSTONE I care not for my spirits, if my legs were not weary.

ROSALIND I could find in my heart to disgrace my man's apparel, and to cry like a woman, but I must comfort the weaker vessel, as doublet-and-hose ought to show itself courageous to petticoat: therefore courage, good Aliena!

CELIA I pray you, bear with me, I cannot go no further.

TOUCHSTONE For my part, I had rather bear with you
10 than bear you: yet I should bear no cross if I did bear you, for I think you have no money in your purse.

ROSALIND Well, this is the Forest of Arden.

TOUCHSTONE Ay, now am I in Arden, the more fool I. When I was at home I was in a better place, but travellers must be content.

Enter Corin and Silvius

ROSALIND

Ay, be so, good Touchstone. – Look you, who comes here:
A young man and an old in solemn talk.

CORIN

That is the way to make her scorn you still.

SILVIUS

O Corin, that thou knewest how I do love her!

CORIN

20 I partly guess, for I have loved ere now.

SILVIUS

No, Corin, being old thou canst not guess,
Though in thy youth thou wast as true a lover
As ever sighed upon a midnight pillow.
But if thy love were ever like to mine –
As sure I think did never man love so –

How many actions most ridiculous
Hast thou been drawn to by thy fantasy?

CORIN
Into a thousand that I have forgotten.

SILVIUS
O, thou didst then never love so heartily.
If thou rememberest not the slightest folly 30
That ever love did make thee run into,
Thou hast not loved.
Or if thou hast not sat as I do now,
Wearing thy hearer in thy mistress' praise,
Thou hast not loved.
Or if thou hast not broke from company
Abruptly, as my passion now makes me,
Thou hast not loved.
O Phebe, Phebe, Phebe! *Exit*

ROSALIND
Alas, poor shepherd, searching of thy wound, 40
I have by hard adventure found mine own.

TOUCHSTONE And I mine. I remember when I was in love I broke my sword upon a stone and bid him take that for coming a-night to Jane Smile, and I remember the kissing of her batler and the cow's dugs that her pretty chopt hands had milked; and I remember the wooing of a peascod instead of her, from whom I took two cods and, giving her them again, said with weeping tears, 'Wear these for my sake.' We that are true lovers run into strange capers; but as all is mortal in nature, so is 50 all nature in love mortal in folly.

ROSALIND Thou speakest wiser than thou art ware of.

TOUCHSTONE Nay, I shall ne'er be ware of mine own wit till I break my shins against it.

ROSALIND
Jove, Jove! This shepherd's passion

Is much upon my fashion.

TOUCHSTONE

And mine, but it grows something stale with me.

CELIA

I pray you, one of you question yond man
If he for gold will give us any food;
60 I faint almost to death.

TOUCHSTONE Holla, you clown!

ROSALIND Peace, fool, he's not thy kinsman.

CORIN Who calls?

TOUCHSTONE Your betters, sir.

CORIN Else are they very wretched.

ROSALIND Peace, I say. Good even to you, friend.

CORIN

And to you, gentle sir, and to you all.

ROSALIND

I prithee, shepherd, if that love or gold
Can in this desert place buy entertainment,
70 Bring us where we may rest ourselves and feed.
Here's a young maid with travail much oppressed,
And faints for succour.

CORIN Fair sir, I pity her,
And wish, for her sake more than for mine own,
My fortunes were more able to relieve her;
But I am shepherd to another man,
And do not shear the fleeces that I graze.
My master is of churlish disposition,
And little recks to find the way to heaven
By doing deeds of hospitality.
80 Besides, his cote, his flocks, and bounds of feed
Are now on sale, and at our sheepcote now,
By reason of his absence, there is nothing
That you will feed on. But what is, come see,
And in my voice most welcome shall you be.

ROSALIND
What is he that shall buy his flock and pasture?

CORIN
That young swain that you saw here but erewhile,
That little cares for buying anything.

ROSALIND
I pray thee, if it stand with honesty,
Buy thou the cottage, pasture, and the flock,
And thou shalt have to pay for it of us. 90

CELIA
And we will mend thy wages: I like this place,
And willingly could waste my time in it.

CORIN
Assuredly the thing is to be sold.
Go with me. If you like upon report
The soil, the profit, and this kind of life,
I will your very faithful feeder be,
And buy it with your gold right suddenly.

Exeunt

Enter Amiens, Jaques and others II.5

AMIENS (*sings*)
Under the greenwood tree,
Who loves to lie with me,
And turn his merry note
Unto the sweet bird's throat:
Come hither, come hither, come hither.
Here shall he see
No enemy
But winter and rough weather.

JAQUES More, more, I prithee, more.

AMIENS It will make you melancholy, Monsieur Jaques. 10

JAQUES I thank it. More, I prithee, more. I can suck

melancholy out of a song, as a weasel sucks eggs. More, I prithee, more.

AMIENS My voice is ragged, I know I cannot please you.

JAQUES I do not desire you to please me, I do desire you to sing. Come, more, another stanzo. Call you 'em 'stanzos'?

AMIENS What you will, Monsieur Jaques.

JAQUES Nay, I care not for their names, they owe me
20 nothing. Will you sing?

AMIENS More at your request than to please myself.

JAQUES Well then, if ever I thank any man, I'll thank you; but that they call 'compliment' is like th'encounter of two dog-apes, and when a man thanks me heartily, methinks I have given him a penny and he renders me the beggarly thanks. Come, sing; and you that will not, hold your tongues.

AMIENS Well, I'll end the song. – Sirs, cover the while: the Duke will drink under this tree. – He hath been all
30 this day to look you.

JAQUES And I have been all this day to avoid him. He is too disputable for my company: I think of as many matters as he, but I give heaven thanks, and make no boast of them. Come, warble, come.

ALL TOGETHER (*sing*)

Who doth ambition shun,
And loves to live i'th'sun,
Seeking the food he eats,
And pleased with what he gets:
Come hither, come hither, come hither.
40 Here shall he see
No enemy
But winter and rough weather.

JAQUES I'll give you a verse to this note, that I made yesterday in despite of my invention.

AMIENS And I'll sing it.

JAQUES Thus it goes:

If it do come to pass
That any man turn ass,
Leaving his wealth and ease,
A stubborn will to please: 50
Ducdame, ducdame, ducdame.
Here shall he see
Gross fools as he,
An if he will come to me.

AMIENS What's that 'ducdame'?

JAQUES 'Tis a Greek invocation, to call fools into a circle. I'll go sleep, if I can; if I cannot, I'll rail against all the first-born of Egypt.

AMIENS And I'll go seek the Duke; his banquet is prepared. *Exeunt* 60

Enter Orlando and Adam II.6

ADAM Dear master, I can go no further. O, I die for food. Here lie I down and measure out my grave. Farewell, kind master.

ORLANDO Why, how now, Adam, no greater heart in thee? Live a little, comfort a little, cheer thyself a little. If this uncouth forest yield anything savage, I will either be food for it or bring it for food to thee. Thy conceit is nearer death than thy powers. (*Raising him*) For my sake be comfortable; hold death a while at the arm's end. I will here be with thee presently, and if I bring thee not 10 something to eat, I will give thee leave to die; but if thou diest before I come, thou art a mocker of my labour. Well said! Thou lookest cheerly, and I'll be with thee quickly. Yet thou liest in the bleak air. Come, I will bear thee to some shelter, and thou shalt not die

for lack of a dinner, if there live anything in this desert.
Cheerly, good Adam! *Exeunt*

II.7 *Enter Duke Senior, Amiens, and Lords, dressed as foresters, or outlaws*

DUKE
I think he be transformed into a beast,
For I can nowhere find him like a man.

FIRST LORD
My lord, he is but even now gone hence.
Here was he merry, hearing of a song.

DUKE
If he, compact of jars, grow musical,
We shall have shortly discord in the spheres.
Go, seek him, tell him I would speak with him.
Enter Jaques

FIRST LORD
He saves my labour by his own approach.

DUKE
Why, how now, Monsieur, what a life is this,
10 That your poor friends must woo your company?
What, you look merrily?

JAQUES
A fool, a fool, I met a fool i'th'forest,
A motley fool – a miserable world! –
As I do live by food, I met a fool,
Who laid him down, and basked him in the sun,
And railed on Lady Fortune in good terms,
In good set terms, and yet a motley fool.
'Good morrow, fool,' quoth I. 'No, sir,' quoth he,
'Call me not fool till heaven hath sent me fortune.'
20 And then he drew a dial from his poke,
And looking on it, with lack-lustre eye,

Says, very wisely, 'It is ten o'clock.'
'Thus we may see', quoth he, 'how the world wags:
'Tis but an hour ago since it was nine,
And after one hour more 'twill be eleven,
And so from hour to hour we ripe, and ripe,
And then from hour to hour we rot, and rot,
And thereby hangs a tale.' When I did hear
The motley fool thus moral on the time,
My lungs began to crow like Chanticleer 30
That fools should be so deep-contemplative;
And I did laugh, sans intermission,
An hour by his dial. O noble fool!
A worthy fool: motley's the only wear!

DUKE
What fool is this?

JAQUES
A worthy fool: one that hath been a courtier,
And says, if ladies be but young and fair,
They have the gift to know it: and in his brain,
Which is as dry as the remainder biscuit
After a voyage, he hath strange places crammed 40
With observation, the which he vents
In mangled forms. O that I were a fool!
I am ambitious for a motley coat.

DUKE
Thou shalt have one.

JAQUES It is my only suit –
Provided that you weed your better judgements
Of all opinion that grows rank in them
That I am wise. I must have liberty
Withal, as large a charter as the wind,
To blow on whom I please, for so fools have;
And they that are most galled with my folly 50
They most must laugh. And why, sir, must they so?

The why is plain as way to parish church.
He that a fool doth very wisely hit
Doth very foolishly, although he smart,
Not to seem senseless of the bob: if not,
The wise man's folly is anatomized
Even by the squandering glances of the fool.
Invest me in my motley; give me leave
To speak my mind, and I will through and through
60 Cleanse the foul body of th'infected world,
If they will patiently receive my medicine.

DUKE

Fie on thee! I can tell what thou wouldst do.

JAQUES

What, for a counter, would I do, but good?

DUKE

Most mischievous foul sin, in chiding sin:
For thou thyself hast been a libertine,
As sensual as the brutish sting itself,
And all th'embossèd sores and headed evils
That thou with licence of free foot hast caught
Wouldst thou disgorge into the general world.

JAQUES

70 Why, who cries out on pride
That can therein tax any private party?
Doth it not flow as hugely as the sea,
Till that the weary very means do ebb?
What woman in the city do I name
When that I say the city woman bears
The cost of princes on unworthy shoulders?
Who can come in and say that I mean her
When such a one as she, such is her neighbour?
Or what is he of basest function,
80 That says his bravery is not on my cost,
Thinking that I mean him, but therein suits
His folly to the mettle of my speech?

There then, how then, what then? Let me see wherein
My tongue hath wronged him: if it do him right,
Then he hath wronged himself; if he be free,
Why then my taxing like a wild-goose flies,
Unclaimed of any man. But who come here?

Enter Orlando

ORLANDO Forbear, and eat no more.

JAQUES Why, I have eat none yet.

ORLANDO
Nor shalt not, till necessity be served. 90

JAQUES
Of what kind should this cock come of?

DUKE
Art thou thus boldened, man, by thy distress
Or else a rude despiser of good manners,
That in civility thou seemest so empty?

ORLANDO
You touched my vein at first: the thorny point
Of bare distress hath ta'en from me the show
Of smooth civility; yet am I inland bred
And know some nurture. But forbear, I say,
He dies that touches any of this fruit
Till I and my affairs are answerèd. 100

JAQUES An you will not be answered with reason, I must die.

DUKE
What would you have? Your gentleness shall force,
More than your force move us to gentleness.

ORLANDO
I almost die for food, and let me have it.

DUKE
Sit down and feed, and welcome to our table.

ORLANDO
Speak you so gently? Pardon me, I pray you.
I thought that all things had been savage here,

And therefore put I on the countenance
110 Of stern commandment. But whate'er you are
That in this desert inaccessible,
Under the shade of melancholy boughs,
Lose and neglect the creeping hours of time:
If ever you have looked on better days;
If ever been where bells have knolled to church;
If ever sat at any good man's feast;
If ever from your eyelids wiped a tear,
And know what 'tis to pity and be pitied,
Let gentleness my strong enforcement be,
120 In the which hope I blush, and hide my sword.

DUKE

True is it that we have seen better days,
And have with holy bell been knolled to church,
And sat at good men's feasts, and wiped our eyes
Of drops that sacred pity hath engendered:
And therefore sit you down in gentleness
And take upon command what help we have
That to your wanting may be ministered.

ORLANDO

Then but forbear your food a little while
Whiles, like a doe, I go to find my fawn
130 And give it food. There is an old poor man
Who after me hath many a weary step
Limped in pure love; till he be first sufficed,
Oppressed with two weak evils, age and hunger,
I will not touch a bit.

DUKE Go find him out
And we will nothing waste till you return.

ORLANDO

I thank ye, and be blessed for your good comfort! *Exit*

DUKE

Thou seest we are not all alone unhappy.

This wide and universal theatre
Presents more woeful pageants than the scene
Wherein we play in.

JAQUES All the world's a stage, 140
And all the men and women merely players;
They have their exits and their entrances,
And one man in his time plays many parts,
His Acts being seven ages. At first the infant,
Mewling and puking in the nurse's arms;
Then, the whining schoolboy, with his satchel
And shining morning face, creeping like snail
Unwillingly to school; and then the lover,
Sighing like furnace, with a woeful ballad
Made to his mistress' eyebrow; then, a soldier, 150
Full of strange oaths, and bearded like the pard,
Jealous in honour, sudden and quick in quarrel,
Seeking the bubble reputation
Even in the cannon's mouth; and then, the justice,
In fair round belly, with good capon lined,
With eyes severe, and beard of formal cut,
Full of wise saws and modern instances,
And so he plays his part; the sixth age shifts
Into the lean and slippered pantaloon,
With spectacles on nose and pouch on side, 160
His youthful hose, well saved, a world too wide
For his shrunk shank, and his big manly voice,
Turning again toward childish treble, pipes
And whistles in his sound; last Scene of all,
That ends this strange eventful history,
Is second childishness, and mere oblivion,
Sans teeth, sans eyes, sans taste, sans everything.

Enter Orlando with Adam

DUKE
Welcome. Set down your venerable burden,

And let him feed.

ORLANDO

I thank you most for him.

170 ADAM So had you need;

I scarce can speak to thank you for myself.

DUKE

Welcome, fall to. I will not trouble you
As yet to question you about your fortunes.
Give us some music and, good cousin, sing.

AMIENS (*sings*)

Blow, blow, thou winter wind,
Thou art not so unkind
As man's ingratitude.
Thy tooth is not so keen,
Because thou art not seen,
180 Although thy breath be rude.
Hey-ho, sing hey-ho, unto the green holly,
Most friendship is feigning, most loving mere folly;
Then hey-ho, the holly,
This life is most jolly.

Freeze, freeze, thou bitter sky
That dost not bite so nigh
As benefits forgot.
Though thou the waters warp,
Thy sting is not so sharp
190 As friend remembered not.
Hey-ho, sing hey-ho, unto the green holly,
Most friendship is feigning, most loving mere folly;
Then hey-ho, the holly,
This life is most jolly.

DUKE

If that you were the good Sir Rowland's son,
As you have whispered faithfully you were,

And as mine eye doth his effigies witness
Most truly limned and living in your face,
Be truly welcome hither. I am the Duke
That loved your father. The residue of your fortune, 200
Go to my cave and tell me. – Good old man,
Thou art right welcome as thy master is. –
Support him by the arm. Give me your hand,
And let me all your fortunes understand. *Exeunt*

*

III.1

Enter Duke Frederick, Lords, and Oliver

DUKE

Not see him since? Sir, sir, that cannot be.
But were I not the better part made mercy,
I should not seek an absent argument
Of my revenge, thou present. But look to it,
Find out thy brother wheresoe'er he is,
Seek him with candle, bring him dead or living
Within this twelvemonth, or turn thou no more
To seek a living in our territory.
Thy lands and all things that thou dost call thine
Worth seizure do we seize into our hands 10
Till thou canst quit thee by thy brother's mouth
Of what we think against thee.

OLIVER

O that your highness knew my heart in this!
I never loved my brother in my life.

DUKE

More villain thou. – Well, push him out of doors,
And let my officers of such a nature
Make an extent upon his house and lands.
Do this expediently, and turn him going. *Exeunt*

III.2 *Enter Orlando*

ORLANDO

Hang there, my verse, in witness of my love,
  And thou, thrice-crownèd queen of night, survey
With thy chaste eye, from thy pale sphere above,
  Thy huntress' name that my full life doth sway.
O Rosalind, these trees shall be my books
  And in their barks my thoughts I'll character
That every eye which in this forest looks
  Shall see thy virtue witnessed everywhere.
Run, run, Orlando, carve on every tree
10 The fair, the chaste, and unexpressive she. *Exit*

Enter Corin and Touchstone

CORIN And how like you this shepherd's life, Master Touchstone?

TOUCHSTONE Truly, shepherd, in respect of itself, it is a good life; but in respect that it is a shepherd's life, it is naught. In respect that it is solitary, I like it very well; but in respect that it is private, it is a very vile life. Now in respect it is in the fields, it pleaseth me well; but in respect it is not in the court, it is tedious. As it is a spare life, look you, it fits my humour well; but as there is no 20 more plenty in it, it goes much against my stomach. Hast any philosophy in thee, shepherd?

CORIN No more but that I know the more one sickens, the worse at ease he is, and that he that wants money, means, and content is without three good friends; that the property of rain is to wet and fire to burn; that good pasture makes fat sheep; and that a great cause of the night is lack of the sun; that he that hath learned no wit by nature nor art may complain of good breeding, or comes of a very dull kindred.

30 TOUCHSTONE Such a one is a natural philosopher. Wast ever in court, shepherd?

CORIN No, truly.

TOUCHSTONE Then thou art damned.

CORIN Nay, I hope.

TOUCHSTONE Truly thou art damned, like an ill-roasted egg all on one side.

CORIN For not being at court? Your reason.

TOUCHSTONE Why, if thou never wast at court, thou never sawest good manners; if thou never sawest good manners, then thy manners must be wicked, and wickedness is sin, and sin is damnation. Thou art in a parlous state, shepherd. 40

CORIN Not a whit, Touchstone. Those that are good manners at the court are as ridiculous in the country as the behaviour of the country is most mockable at the court. You told me you salute not at the court but you kiss your hands; that courtesy would be uncleanly if courtiers were shepherds.

TOUCHSTONE Instance, briefly; come, instance.

CORIN Why, we are still handling our ewes, and their fells you know are greasy. 50

TOUCHSTONE Why, do not your courtier's hands sweat? And is not the grease of a mutton as wholesome as the sweat of a man? Shallow, shallow. A better instance, I say; come.

CORIN Besides, our hands are hard.

TOUCHSTONE Your lips will feel them the sooner. Shallow, again. A more sounder instance; come.

CORIN And they are often tarred over with the surgery of our sheep; and would you have us kiss tar? The courtier's hands are perfumed with civet. 60

TOUCHSTONE Most shallow man! Thou worms' meat, in respect of a good piece of flesh indeed! Learn of the wise and perpend: civet is of a baser birth than tar, the very uncleanly flux of a cat. Mend the instance, shepherd.

CORIN You have too courtly a wit for me; I'll rest.

TOUCHSTONE Wilt thou rest damned? God help thee, shallow man! God make incision in thee, thou art raw!

CORIN Sir, I am a true labourer: I earn that I eat, get
70 that I wear, owe no man hate, envy no man's happiness, glad of other men's good, content with my harm; and the greatest of my pride is to see my ewes graze and my lambs suck.

TOUCHSTONE That is another simple sin in you, to bring the ewes and the rams together and to offer to get your living by the copulation of cattle; to be bawd to a bell-wether, and to betray a she-lamb of a twelvemonth to a crooked-pated, old, cuckoldly ram, out of all reasonable match. If thou beest not damned for this, the devil
80 himself will have no shepherds. I cannot see else how thou shouldst 'scape.

CORIN Here comes young Master Ganymede, my new mistress's brother.

Enter Rosalind

ROSALIND (*reads*)

From the east to western Ind,
No jewel is like Rosalind.
Her worth being mounted on the wind
Through all the world bears Rosalind.
All the pictures fairest lined
Are but black to Rosalind.
90 *Let no face be kept in mind*
But the fair of Rosalind.

TOUCHSTONE I'll rhyme you so eight years together, dinners and suppers and sleeping-hours excepted: it is the right butter-women's rank to market.

ROSALIND Out, fool!

TOUCHSTONE For a taste:

If a hart do lack a hind,

Let him seek out Rosalind.
If the cat will after kind,
So be sure will Rosalind. 100
Wintered garments must be lined,
So must slender Rosalind.
They that reap must sheaf and bind,
Then to cart with Rosalind.
Sweetest nut hath sourest rind,
Such a nut is Rosalind.
He that sweetest rose will find,
Must find love's prick and Rosalind.

This is the very false gallop of verses. Why do you infect yourself with them? 110

ROSALIND Peace, you dull fool, I found them on a tree.

TOUCHSTONE Truly, the tree yields bad fruit.

ROSALIND I'll graff it with you, and then I shall graff it with a medlar; then it will be the earliest fruit i'th'country: for you'll be rotten ere you be half ripe, and that's the right virtue of the medlar.

TOUCHSTONE You have said; but whether wisely or no, let the forest judge.

Enter Celia with a writing

ROSALIND Peace, here comes my sister, reading. Stand aside. 120

CELIA (*reads*)

Why should this a desert be?
For it is unpeopled? No,
Tongues I'll hang on every tree,
That shall civil sayings show.
Some, how brief the life of man
Runs his erring pilgrimage,
That the stretching of a span
Buckles in his sum of age;
Some, of violated vows

130 *'Twixt the souls of friend and friend;*
But upon the fairest boughs,
Or at every sentence end,
Will I 'Rosalinda' write,
Teaching all that read to know
The quintessence of every sprite
Heaven would in little show.
Therefore Heaven Nature charged
That one body should be filled
With all graces wide-enlarged.
140 *Nature presently distilled*
Helen's cheek, but not her heart,
Cleopatra's majesty,
Atalanta's better part,
Sad Lucretia's modesty.
Thus Rosalind of many parts
By heavenly synod was devised,
Of many faces, eyes, and hearts,
To have the touches dearest prized.
Heaven would that she these gifts should have,
150 *And I to live and die her slave.*

ROSALIND O most gentle Jupiter, what tedious homily of love have you wearied your parishioners withal, and never cried 'Have patience, good people!'

CELIA How now? Back, friends. – Shepherd, go off a little. – Go with him, sirrah.

TOUCHSTONE Come, shepherd, let us make an honourable retreat, though not with bag and baggage, yet with scrip and scrippage.

Exit Touchstone, with Corin

CELIA Didst thou hear these verses?

160 ROSALIND O, yes, I heard them all, and more too, for some of them had in them more feet than the verses would bear.

CELIA That's no matter: the feet might bear the verses.

ROSALIND Ay, but the feet were lame, and could not bear themselves without the verse, and therefore stood lamely in the verse.

CELIA But didst thou hear without wondering how thy name should be hanged and carved upon these trees?

ROSALIND I was seven of the nine days out of the wonder before you came; for look here what I found on a palm-tree. I was never so be-rhymed since Pythagoras' time that I was an Irish rat, which I can hardly remember. 170

CELIA Trow you who hath done this?

ROSALIND Is it a man?

CELIA And a chain that you once wore about his neck! Change you colour?

ROSALIND I prithee, who?

CELIA O Lord, Lord, it is a hard matter for friends to meet; but mountains may be removed with earthquakes and so encounter. 180

ROSALIND Nay, but who is it?

CELIA Is it possible?

ROSALIND Nay, I prithee now with most petitionary vehemence, tell me who it is.

CELIA O wonderful, wonderful, and most wonderful wonderful, and yet again wonderful, and after that out of all whooping!

ROSALIND Good my complexion! Dost thou think, though I am caparisoned like a man, I have a doublet and hose in my disposition? One inch of delay more is a South Sea of discovery. I prithee tell me who is it quickly, and speak apace. I would thou couldst stammer, that thou mightst pour this concealed man out of thy mouth as wine comes out of a narrow-mouthed bottle: either too much at once, or none at all. I prithee take the cork out of thy mouth, that I may drink thy tidings. 190

CELIA So you may put a man in your belly.

ROSALIND Is he of God's making? What manner of man? Is his head worth a hat? Or his chin worth a
200 beard?

CELIA Nay, he hath but a little beard.

ROSALIND Why, God will send more, if the man will be thankful. Let me stay the growth of his beard, if thou delay me not the knowledge of his chin.

CELIA It is young Orlando, that tripped up the wrestler's heels and your heart, both in an instant.

ROSALIND Nay, but the devil take mocking; speak sad brow and true maid.

CELIA I'faith, coz, 'tis he.

210 ROSALIND Orlando?

CELIA Orlando.

ROSALIND Alas the day, what shall I do with my doublet and hose? What did he when thou sawest him? What said he? How looked he? Wherein went he? What makes he here? Did he ask for me? Where remains he? How parted he with thee? And when shalt thou see him again? Answer me in one word.

CELIA You must borrow me Gargantua's mouth first: 'tis a word too great for any mouth of this age's size.
220 To say 'ay' and 'no' to these particulars is more than to answer in a catechism.

ROSALIND But doth he know that I am in this forest and in man's apparel? Looks he as freshly as he did the day he wrestled?

CELIA It is as easy to count atomies as to resolve the propositions of a lover; but take a taste of my finding him, and relish it with good observance. I found him under a tree like a dropped acorn.

ROSALIND It may well be called Jove's tree, when it
230 drops such fruit.

CELIA Give me audience, good madam.

ROSALIND Proceed.

CELIA There lay he, stretched along like a wounded knight.

ROSALIND Though it be pity to see such a sight, it well becomes the ground.

CELIA Cry 'holla' to thy tongue, I prithee; it curvets unseasonably. He was furnished like a hunter.

ROSALIND O ominous! He comes to kill my heart.

CELIA I would sing my song without a burden. Thou bringest me out of tune. 240

ROSALIND Do you not know I am a woman? When I think, I must speak. Sweet, say on.

Enter Orlando and Jaques

CELIA You bring me out. Soft, comes he not here?

ROSALIND 'Tis he. Slink by, and note him.

Celia and Rosalind stand back

JAQUES I thank you for your company, but, good faith, I had as lief have been myself alone.

ORLANDO And so had I; but yet, for fashion sake, I thank you too for your society.

JAQUES God buy you, let's meet as little as we can. 250

ORLANDO I do desire we may be better strangers.

JAQUES I pray you, mar no more trees with writing love-songs in their barks.

ORLANDO I pray you, mar no moe of my verses with reading them ill-favouredly.

JAQUES Rosalind is your love's name?

ORLANDO Yes, just.

JAQUES I do not like her name.

ORLANDO There was no thought of pleasing you when she was christened. 260

JAQUES What stature is she of?

ORLANDO Just as high as my heart.

JAQUES You are full of pretty answers: have you not been acquainted with goldsmiths' wives, and conned them out of rings?

ORLANDO Not so; but I answer you right painted cloth, from whence you have studied your questions.

JAQUES You have a nimble wit; I think 'twas made of Atalanta's heels. Will you sit down with me, and we two
270 will rail against our mistress the world, and all our misery?

ORLANDO I will chide no breather in the world but myself, against whom I know most faults.

JAQUES The worst fault you have is to be in love.

ORLANDO 'Tis a fault I will not change for your best virtue. I am weary of you.

JAQUES By my troth, I was seeking for a fool when I found you.

ORLANDO He is drowned in the brook; look but in and
280 you shall see him.

JAQUES There I shall see mine own figure.

ORLANDO Which I take to be either a fool or a cipher.

JAQUES I'll tarry no longer with you. Farewell, good Signor Love.

ORLANDO I am glad of your departure. Adieu, good Monsieur Melancholy.

Exit Jaques

ROSALIND (*to Celia*) I will speak to him like a saucy lackey, and under that habit play the knave with him. – Do you hear, forester?

290 ORLANDO Very well. What would you?

ROSALIND I pray you, what is't o'clock?

ORLANDO You should ask me what time o'day: there's no clock in the forest.

ROSALIND Then there is no true lover in the forest, else sighing every minute and groaning every hour would detect the lazy foot of Time as well as a clock.

ORLANDO And why not the swift foot of Time? Had not that been as proper?

ROSALIND By no means, sir: Time travels in divers paces with divers persons. I'll tell you who Time ambles withal, who Time trots withal, who Time gallops withal, and who he stands still withal. 300

ORLANDO I prithee, who doth he trot withal?

ROSALIND Marry, he trots hard with a young maid between the contract of her marriage and the day it is solemnized. If the interim be but a se'nnight, Time's pace is so hard that it seems the length of seven year.

ORLANDO Who ambles Time withal?

ROSALIND With a priest that lacks Latin, and a rich man that hath not the gout: for the one sleeps easily because he cannot study, and the other lives merrily because he feels no pain, the one lacking the burden of lean and wasteful learning, the other knowing no burden of heavy tedious penury. These Time ambles withal. 310

ORLANDO Who doth he gallop withal?

ROSALIND With a thief to the gallows: for though he go as softly as foot can fall, he thinks himself too soon there.

ORLANDO Who stays it still withal?

ROSALIND With lawyers in the vacation: for they sleep between term and term, and then they perceive not how Time moves. 320

ORLANDO Where dwell you, pretty youth?

ROSALIND With this shepherdess, my sister, here in the skirts of the forest, like fringe upon a petticoat.

ORLANDO Are you native of this place?

ROSALIND As the cony that you see dwell where she is kindled.

ORLANDO Your accent is something finer than you could

330 purchase in so removed a dwelling.

ROSALIND I have been told so of many; but indeed an old religious uncle of mine taught me to speak, who was in his youth an inland man – one that knew courtship too well, for there he fell in love. I have heard him read many lectures against it, and I thank God I am not a woman, to be touched with so many giddy offences as he hath generally taxed their whole sex withal.

ORLANDO Can you remember any of the principal evils that he laid to the charge of women?

340 ROSALIND There were none principal, they were all like one another as halfpence are, every one fault seeming monstrous till his fellow-fault came to match it.

ORLANDO I prithee, recount some of them.

ROSALIND No, I will not cast away my physic but on those that are sick. There is a man haunts the forest that abuses our young plants with carving 'Rosalind' on their barks; hangs odes upon hawthorns, and elegies on brambles; all, forsooth, deifying the name of Rosalind. If I could meet that fancy-monger, I would give him 350 some good counsel, for he seems to have the quotidian of love upon him.

ORLANDO I am he that is so love-shaked. I pray you, tell me your remedy.

ROSALIND There is none of my uncle's marks upon you. He taught me how to know a man in love; in which cage of rushes I am sure you are not prisoner.

ORLANDO What were his marks?

ROSALIND A lean cheek, which you have not; a blue eye and sunken, which you have not; an unquestionable 360 spirit, which you have not; a beard neglected, which you have not – but I pardon you for that, for simply your having in beard is a younger brother's revenue. Then your hose should be ungartered, your bonnet unbanded, your sleeve unbuttoned, your shoe untied, and everything about you demonstrating a careless desolation. But you are no such man: you are rather point-device in your accoutrements, as loving yourself, than seeming the lover of any other.

ORLANDO Fair youth, I would I could make thee believe I love. 370

ROSALIND Me believe it? You may as soon make her that you love believe it, which I warrant she is apter to do than to confess she does: that is one of the points in the which women still give the lie to their consciences. But in good sooth, are you he that hangs the verses on the trees, wherein Rosalind is so admired?

ORLANDO I swear to thee, youth, by the white hand of Rosalind, I am that he, that unfortunate he.

ROSALIND But are you so much in love as your rhymes speak? 380

ORLANDO Neither rhyme nor reason can express how much.

ROSALIND Love is merely a madness and, I tell you, deserves as well a dark house and a whip as madmen do; and the reason why they are not so punished and cured is that the lunacy is so ordinary that the whippers are in love too. Yet I profess curing it by counsel.

ORLANDO Did you ever cure any so?

ROSALIND Yes, one, and in this manner. He was to imagine me his love, his mistress; and I set him every 390 day to woo me. At which time would I, being but a moonish youth, grieve, be effeminate, changeable, longing and liking, proud, fantastical, apish, shallow, inconstant, full of tears, full of smiles; for every passion something, and for no passion truly anything, as boys and women are for the most part cattle of this colour; would now like him, now loathe him; then entertain

him, then forswear him; now weep for him, then spit at him; that I drave my suitor from his mad humour of
400 love to a living humour of madness – which was, to forswear the full stream of the world and to live in a nook merely monastic. And thus I cured him, and this way will I take upon me to wash your liver as clean as a sound sheep's heart, that there shall not be one spot of love in't.

ORLANDO I would not be cured, youth.

ROSALIND I would cure you, if you would but call me 'Rosalind', and come every day to my cote, and woo me.

ORLANDO Now, by the faith of my love, I will. Tell me
410 where it is.

ROSALIND Go with me to it and I'll show it you: and by the way you shall tell me where in the forest you live. Will you go?

ORLANDO With all my heart, good youth.

ROSALIND Nay, you must call me 'Rosalind'. – Come, sister, will you go? *Exeunt*

III.3 *Enter Touchstone and Audrey, followed by Jaques*

TOUCHSTONE Come apace, good Audrey. I will fetch up your goats, Audrey. And now, Audrey, am I the man yet? Doth my simple feature content you?

AUDREY Your features, Lord warrant us! What features?

TOUCHSTONE I am here with thee and thy goats, as the most capricious poet, honest Ovid, was among the Goths.

JAQUES (*aside*) O knowledge ill-inhabited, worse than Jove in a thatched house!

10 TOUCHSTONE When a man's verses cannot be understood, nor a man's good wit seconded with the forward child Understanding, it strikes a man more dead than a great

reckoning in a little room. Truly, I would the gods had made thee poetical.

AUDREY I do not know what 'poetical' is. Is it honest in deed and word? Is it a true thing?

TOUCHSTONE No, truly: for the truest poetry is the most feigning; and lovers are given to poetry; and what they swear in poetry may be said as lovers they do feign.

AUDREY Do you wish then that the gods had made me poetical? 20

TOUCHSTONE I do, truly: for thou swearest to me thou art honest; now, if thou wert a poet, I might have some hope thou didst feign.

AUDREY Would you not have me honest?

TOUCHSTONE No, truly, unless thou wert hard-favoured: for honesty coupled to beauty is to have honey a sauce to sugar.

JAQUES (*aside*) A material fool!

AUDREY Well, I am not fair, and therefore I pray the gods make me honest. 30

TOUCHSTONE Truly, and to cast away honesty upon a foul slut were to put good meat into an unclean dish.

AUDREY I am not a slut, though I thank the gods I am foul.

TOUCHSTONE Well, praised be the gods for thy foulness; sluttishness may come hereafter. But be it as it may be, I will marry thee; and to that end, I have been with Sir Oliver Martext, the vicar of the next village, who hath promised to meet me in this place of the forest and to couple us. 40

JAQUES (*aside*) I would fain see this meeting.

AUDREY Well, the gods give us joy.

TOUCHSTONE Amen. A man may, if he were of a fearful heart, stagger in this attempt; for here we have no temple but the wood, no assembly but horn-beasts. But what

though? Courage! As horns are odious, they are necessary. It is said, 'Many a man knows no end of his goods'. Right! Many a man has good horns, and knows no end
50 of them. Well, that is the dowry of his wife, 'tis none of his own getting. Horns? Even so. Poor men alone? No, no, the noblest deer hath them as huge as the rascal. Is the single man therefore blessed? No. As a walled town is more worthier than a village, so is the forehead of a married man more honourable than the bare brow of a bachelor; and by how much defence is better than no skill, by so much is a horn more precious than to want.

Enter Sir Oliver Martext

Here comes Sir Oliver. – Sir Oliver Martext, you are
60 well met. Will you dispatch us here under this tree, or shall we go with you to your chapel?

SIR OLIVER Is there none here to give the woman?

TOUCHSTONE I will not take her on gift of any man.

SIR OLIVER Truly, she must be given, or the marriage is not lawful.

JAQUES (*coming forward*) Proceed, proceed; I'll give her.

TOUCHSTONE Good even, good Master What-ye-call't: how do you, sir? You are very well met. God 'ild you for your last company, I am very glad to see you.
70 Even a toy in hand here, sir. Nay, pray be covered.

JAQUES Will you be married, motley?

TOUCHSTONE As the ox hath his bow, sir, the horse his curb, and the falcon her bells, so man hath his desires; and as pigeons bill, so wedlock would be nibbling.

JAQUES And will you, being a man of your breeding, be married under a bush like a beggar? Get you to church, and have a good priest that can tell you what marriage is. This fellow will but join you together as they join wainscot; then one of you will prove a shrunk panel and, like green timber, warp, warp. 80

TOUCHSTONE I am not in the mind but I were better to be married of him than of another, for he is not like to marry me well; and not being well married, it will be a good excuse for me hereafter to leave my wife.

JAQUES Go thou with me, and let me counsel thee.

TOUCHSTONE Come, sweet Audrey, we must be married, or we must live in bawdry. Farewell, good Master Oliver. Not

O sweet Oliver,
O brave Oliver, 90
Leave me not behind thee

but

Wind away,
Be gone, I say,
I will not to wedding with thee.

SIR OLIVER (*aside*) 'Tis no matter; ne'er a fantastical knave of them all shall flout me out of my calling.

Exeunt

Enter Rosalind and Celia III.4

ROSALIND Never talk to me, I will weep.

CELIA Do, I prithee, but yet have the grace to consider that tears do not become a man.

ROSALIND But have I not cause to weep?

CELIA As good cause as one would desire; therefore weep.

ROSALIND His very hair is of the dissembling colour.

CELIA Something browner than Judas's. Marry, his kisses are Judas's own children.

ROSALIND I'faith, his hair is of a good colour.

CELIA An excellent colour: your chestnut was ever the only colour. 10

ROSALIND And his kissing is as full of sanctity as the touch of holy bread.

CELIA He hath bought a pair of cast lips of Diana. A nun of winter's sisterhood kisses not more religiously; the very ice of chastity is in them.

ROSALIND But why did he swear he would come this morning, and comes not?

CELIA Nay, certainly, there is no truth in him.

20 ROSALIND Do you think so?

CELIA Yes, I think he is not a pick-purse nor a horse-stealer, but for his verity in love I do think him as concave as a covered goblet or a worm-eaten nut.

ROSALIND Not true in love?

CELIA Yes, when he is in – but I think he is not in.

ROSALIND You have heard him swear downright he was.

CELIA 'Was' is not 'is'. Besides, the oath of lover is no stronger than the word of a tapster: they are both the confirmer of false reckonings. He attends here in the

30 forest on the Duke your father.

ROSALIND I met the Duke yesterday and had much question with him. He asked me of what parentage I was. I told him, of as good as he – so he laughed and let me go. But what talk we of fathers, when there is such a man as Orlando?

CELIA O, that's a brave man! He writes brave verses, speaks brave words, swears brave oaths and breaks them bravely, quite traverse, athwart the heart of his lover, as a puisny tilter that spurs his horse but on one

40 side breaks his staff like a noble goose. But all's brave that youth mounts and folly guides. Who comes here?

Enter Corin

CORIN

Mistress and master, you have oft inquired
After the shepherd that complained of love,
Who you saw sitting by me on the turf,
Praising the proud disdainful shepherdess
That was his mistress.

CELIA Well: and what of him?

CORIN

If you will see a pageant truly played,
Between the pale complexion of true love
And the red glow of scorn and proud disdain,
Go hence a little and I shall conduct you, 50
If you will mark it.

ROSALIND O come, let us remove;
The sight of lovers feedeth those in love.
Bring us to this sight, and you shall say
I'll prove a busy actor in their play. *Exeunt*

Enter Silvius and Phebe III.5

SILVIUS

Sweet Phebe, do not scorn me, do not, Phebe.
Say that you love me not, but say not so
In bitterness. The common executioner,
Whose heart th'accustomed sight of death makes hard,
Falls not the axe upon the humbled neck
But first begs pardon: will you sterner be
Than he that dies and lives by bloody drops?

Enter Rosalind, Celia, and Corin, unobserved

PHEBE

I would not be thy executioner.
I fly thee, for I would not injure thee.
Thou tellest me there is murder in mine eye: 10
'Tis pretty, sure, and very probable,
That eyes, that are the frail'st and softest things,
Who shut their coward gates on atomies,
Should be called tyrants, butchers, murderers!
Now I do frown on thee with all my heart,
And if mine eyes can wound, now let them kill thee.
Now counterfeit to swoon, why now fall down,
Or if thou canst not, O for shame, for shame,

Lie not, to say mine eyes are murderers!
20 Now show the wound mine eye hath made in thee.
Scratch thee but with a pin, and there remains
Some scar of it; lean upon a rush,
The cicatrice and capable impressure
Thy palm some moment keeps; but now mine eyes,
Which I have darted at thee, hurt thee not,
Nor, I am sure, there is no force in eyes
That can do hurt.

SILVIUS O dear Phebe,
If ever – as that ever may be near –
You meet in some fresh cheek the power of fancy,
30 Then shall you know the wounds invisible
That love's keen arrows make.

PHEBE But till that time
Come not thou near me; and when that time comes,
Afflict me with thy mocks, pity me not,
As till that time I shall not pity thee.

ROSALIND (*coming forward*)
And why, I pray you? Who might be your mother,
That you insult, exult and all at once
Over the wretched? What, though you have no
beauty –
As, by my faith, I see no more in you
Than without candle may go dark to bed –
40 Must you be therefore proud and pitiless?
Why, what means this? Why do you look on me?
I see no more in you than in the ordinary
Of nature's sale-work. 'Od's my little life,
I think she means to tangle my eyes too!
No, faith, proud mistress, hope not after it:
'Tis not your inky brows, your black silk hair,
Your bugle eyeballs, nor your cheek of cream
That can entame my spirits to your worship.

You foolish shepherd, wherefore do you follow her,
Like foggy south, puffing with wind and rain? 50
You are a thousand times a properer man
Than she a woman. 'Tis such fools as you
That makes the world full of ill-favoured children.
'Tis not her glass but you that flatters her,
And out of you she sees herself more proper
Than any of her lineaments can show her.
But, mistress, know yourself; down on your knees
And thank heaven, fasting, for a good man's love!
For I must tell you friendly in your ear,
Sell when you can, you are not for all markets. 60
Cry the man mercy, love him, take his offer.
Foul is most foul, being foul to be a scoffer.
So take her to thee, shepherd. Fare you well.

PHEBE
Sweet youth, I pray you chide a year together;
I had rather hear you chide than this man woo.

ROSALIND (*to Phebe*) He's fallen in love with your foulness,
(*to Silvius*) and she'll fall in love with my anger. If it
be so, as fast as she answers thee with frowning looks,
I'll sauce her with bitter words. (*To Phebe*) Why look
you so upon me? 70

PHEBE
For no ill will I bear you.

ROSALIND
I pray you, do not fall in love with me,
For I am falser than vows made in wine.
Besides, I like you not. (*To Silvius*) If you will know
my house,
'Tis at the tuft of olives here hard by. –
Will you go, sister? – Shepherd, ply her hard. –
Come, sister. – Shepherdess, look on him better,
And be not proud, though all the world could see,

None could be so abused in sight as he.
80 Come, to our flock.

Exit Rosalind, with Celia and Corin

PHEBE

Dead Shepherd, now I find thy saw of might,
'Who ever loved that loved not at first sight?'

SILVIUS

Sweet Phebe –

PHEBE Ha, what sayest thou, Silvius?

SILVIUS

Sweet Phebe, pity me.

PHEBE

Why, I am sorry for thee, gentle Silvius.

SILVIUS

Wherever sorrow is, relief would be.
If you do sorrow at my grief in love,
By giving love, your sorrow and my grief
Were both extermined.

PHEBE

90 Thou hast my love; is not that neighbourly?

SILVIUS

I would have you.

PHEBE Why, that were covetousness.
Silvius, the time was that I hated thee,
And yet it is not that I bear thee love;
But since that thou canst talk of love so well,
Thy company, which erst was irksome to me,
I will endure, and I'll employ thee too.
But do not look for further recompense
Than thine own gladness that thou art employed.

SILVIUS

So holy and so perfect is my love,
100 And I in such a poverty of grace,
That I shall think it a most plenteous crop

To glean the broken ears after the man
That the main harvest reaps. Loose now and then
A scattered smile, and that I'll live upon.

PHEBE

Knowest thou the youth that spoke to me erewhile?

SILVIUS

Not very well, but I have met him oft,
And he hath bought the cottage and the bounds
That the old carlot once was master of.

PHEBE

Think not I love him, though I ask for him.
'Tis but a peevish boy. Yet he talks well. 110
But what care I for words? Yet words do well
When he that speaks them pleases those that hear.
It is a pretty youth – not very pretty –
But, sure, he's proud – and yet his pride becomes him.
He'll make a proper man. The best thing in him
Is his complexion; and faster than his tongue
Did make offence, his eye did heal it up.
He is not very tall – yet for his years he's tall.
His leg is but so so – and yet 'tis well.
There was a pretty redness in his lip, 120
A little riper and more lusty red
Than that mixed in his cheek; 'twas just the difference
Betwixt the constant red and mingled damask.
There be some women, Silvius, had they marked him
In parcels, as I did, would have gone near
To fall in love with him: but, for my part,
I love him not, nor hate him not; and yet
I have more cause to hate him than to love him,
For what had he to do to chide at me?
He said mine eyes were black and my hair black, 130
And, now I am remembered, scorned at me;
I marvel why I answered not again.

But that's all one: omittance is no quittance;
I'll write to him a very taunting letter,
And thou shalt bear it – wilt thou, Silvius?

SILVIUS
Phebe, with all my heart.

PHEBE I'll write it straight:
The matter's in my head and in my heart.
I will be bitter with him and passing short.
Go with me, Silvius. *Exeunt*

*

IV.1 *Enter Rosalind, Celia, and Jaques*

JAQUES I prithee, pretty youth, let me be better acquainted with thee.

ROSALIND They say you are a melancholy fellow.

JAQUES I am so: I do love it better than laughing.

ROSALIND Those that are in extremity of either are abominable fellows, and betray themselves to every modern censure worse than drunkards.

JAQUES Why, 'tis good to be sad and say nothing.

ROSALIND Why then, 'tis good to be a post.

JAQUES I have neither the scholar's melancholy, which is emulation; nor the musician's, which is fantastical; nor the courtier's, which is proud; nor the soldier's, which is ambitious; nor the lawyer's, which is politic; nor the lady's, which is nice; nor the lover's, which is all these: but it is a melancholy of mine own, compounded of many simples, extracted from many objects, and indeed the sundry contemplation of my travels, in which my often rumination wraps me in a most humorous sadness.

ROSALIND A traveller! By my faith, you have great reason to be sad. I fear you have sold your own lands to see other men's; then, to have seen much and to have nothing is to have rich eyes and poor hands.

JAQUES Yes, I have gained my experience.

Enter Orlando

ROSALIND And your experience makes you sad. I had rather have a fool to make me merry than experience to make me sad – and to travail for it too!

ORLANDO
Good day, and happiness, dear Rosalind!

JAQUES Nay then, God buy you, an you talk in blank verse. (*Going*)

ROSALIND (*as he goes*) Farewell, Monsieur Traveller. Look you lisp and wear strange suits; disable all the benefits 30 of your own country; be out of love with your nativity, and almost chide God for making you that countenance you are; or I will scarce think you have swam in a gondola. – Why, how now, Orlando, where have you been all this while? You a lover! An you serve me such another trick, never come in my sight more.

ORLANDO My fair Rosalind, I come within an hour of my promise.

ROSALIND Break an hour's promise in love? He that will divide a minute into a thousand parts, and break but a 40 part of the thousandth part of a minute in the affairs of love, it may be said of him that Cupid hath clapped him o'th'shoulder, but I'll warrant him heart-whole.

ORLANDO Pardon me, dear Rosalind.

ROSALIND Nay, an you be so tardy come no more in my sight; I had as lief be wooed of a snail.

ORLANDO Of a snail?

ROSALIND Ay, of a snail: for though he comes slowly, he carries his house on his head – a better jointure, I think, than you make a woman. Besides, he brings his destiny 50 with him.

ORLANDO What's that?

ROSALIND Why, horns; which such as you are fain to be beholding to your wives for. But he comes armed in his fortune, and prevents the slander of his wife.

ORLANDO Virtue is no horn-maker; and my Rosalind is virtuous.

ROSALIND And I am your Rosalind.

CELIA It pleases him to call you so; but he hath a Rosalind
60 of a better leer than you.

ROSALIND Come, woo me, woo me: for now I am in a holiday humour, and like enough to consent. What would you say to me now, an I were your very, very Rosalind?

ORLANDO I would kiss before I spoke.

ROSALIND Nay, you were better speak first, and when you were gravelled for lack of matter, you might take occasion to kiss. Very good orators, when they are out, they will spit, and for lovers lacking – God warn us! – matter, the
70 cleanliest shift is to kiss.

ORLANDO How if the kiss be denied?

ROSALIND Then she puts you to entreaty, and there begins new matter.

ORLANDO Who could be out, being before his beloved mistress?

ROSALIND Marry, that should you if I were your mistress, or I should think my honesty ranker than my wit.

ORLANDO What, of my suit?

ROSALIND Not out of your apparel, and yet out of your
80 suit. Am not I your Rosalind?

ORLANDO I take some joy to say you are, because I would be talking of her.

ROSALIND Well, in her person, I say I will not have you.

ORLANDO Then, in mine own person, I die.

ROSALIND No, faith, die by attorney. The poor world is almost six thousand years old, and in all this time there was not any man died in his own person, videlicet, in a love-cause. Troilus had his brains dashed out with a Grecian club, yet he did what he could to die before, and he is one of the patterns of love. Leander, he would 90 have lived many a fair year though Hero had turned nun, if it had not been for a hot midsummer night: for, good youth, he went but forth to wash him in the Hellespont and being taken with the cramp was drowned, and the foolish chroniclers of that age found it was 'Hero of Sestos'. But these are all lies; men have died from time to time and worms have eaten them, but not for love.

ORLANDO I would not have my right Rosalind of this mind, for I protest her frown might kill me. 100

ROSALIND By this hand, it will not kill a fly. But come, now I will be your Rosalind in a more coming-on disposition; and ask me what you will, I will grant it.

ORLANDO Then love me, Rosalind.

ROSALIND Yes, faith will I, Fridays and Saturdays and all.

ORLANDO And wilt thou have me?

ROSALIND Ay, and twenty such.

ORLANDO What sayest thou?

ROSALIND Are you not good? 110

ORLANDO I hope so.

ROSALIND Why then, can one desire too much of a good thing? Come, sister, you shall be the priest and marry us. – Give me your hand, Orlando. – What do you say, sister?

ORLANDO Pray thee, marry us.

CELIA I cannot say the words.

ROSALIND You must begin 'Will you, Orlando'.

CELIA Go to. – Will you, Orlando, have to wife this Rosalind? 120

ORLANDO I will.

ROSALIND Ay, but when?

ORLANDO Why, now, as fast as she can marry us.

ROSALIND Then you must say 'I take thee, Rosalind, for wife.'

ORLANDO I take thee, Rosalind, for wife.

ROSALIND I might ask you for your commission, but I do take thee, Orlando, for my husband. There's a girl goes before the priest, and certainly a woman's thought
130 runs before her actions.

ORLANDO So do all thoughts, they are winged.

ROSALIND Now tell me how long you would have her after you have possessed her.

ORLANDO For ever and a day.

ROSALIND Say 'a day' without the 'ever'. No, no, Orlando, men are April when they woo, December when they wed; maids are May when they are maids, but the sky changes when they are wives. I will be more jealous of thee than a Barbary cock-pigeon over his hen, more
140 clamorous than a parrot against rain, more new-fangled than an ape, more giddy in my desires than a monkey; I will weep for nothing, like Diana in the fountain, and I will do that when you are disposed to be merry; I will laugh like a hyen, and that when thou art inclined to sleep.

ORLANDO But will my Rosalind do so?

ROSALIND By my life, she will do as I do.

ORLANDO O, but she is wise.

ROSALIND Or else she could not have the wit to do this.
150 The wiser, the waywarder. Make the doors upon a woman's wit, and it will out at the casement; shut that, and 'twill out at the key-hole; stop that, 'twill fly with the smoke out at the chimney.

ORLANDO A man that had a wife with such a wit, he might say 'Wit, whither wilt?'

ROSALIND Nay, you might keep that check for it, till you met your wife's wit going to your neighbour's bed.

ORLANDO And what wit could wit have to excuse that?

ROSALIND Marry, to say she came to seek you there. You shall never take her without her answer, unless you take 160 her without her tongue. O, that woman that cannot make her fault her husband's occasion, let her never nurse her child herself, for she will breed it like a fool.

ORLANDO For these two hours, Rosalind, I will leave thee.

ROSALIND Alas, dear love, I cannot lack thee two hours!

ORLANDO I must attend the Duke at dinner. By two o'clock I will be with thee again.

ROSALIND Ay, go your ways, go your ways: I knew what you would prove, my friends told me as much, and I thought no less. That flattering tongue of yours won 170 me. 'Tis but one cast away, and so, come death. Two o'clock is your hour?

ORLANDO Ay, sweet Rosalind.

ROSALIND By my troth, and in good earnest, and so God mend me, and by all pretty oaths that are not dangerous, if you break one jot of your promise, or come one minute behind your hour, I will think you the most pathetical break-promise, and the most hollow lover, and the most unworthy of her you call Rosalind, that may be chosen out of the gross band of the unfaithful. Therefore, 180 beware my censure, and keep your promise.

ORLANDO With no less religion than if thou wert indeed my Rosalind. So, adieu.

ROSALIND Well, Time is the old justice that examines all such offenders, and let Time try. Adieu! *Exit Orlando*

CELIA You have simply misused our sex in your love-prate. We must have your doublet and hose plucked over your head, and show the world what the bird hath done to her own nest.

190 ROSALIND O coz, coz, coz, my pretty little coz, that thou didst know how many fathom deep I am in love! But it cannot be sounded: my affection hath an unknown bottom, like the Bay of Portugal.

CELIA Or rather, bottomless, that as fast as you pour affection in, it runs out.

ROSALIND No, that same wicked bastard of Venus, that was begot of thought, conceived of spleen, and born of madness, that blind rascally boy that abuses everyone's eyes because his own are out, let him be judge how 200 deep I am in love. I'll tell thee, Aliena, I cannot be out of the sight of Orlando: I'll go find a shadow and sigh till he come.

CELIA And I'll sleep. *Exeunt*

IV.2 *Enter Jaques, and Lords dressed as foresters*

JAQUES Which is he that killed the deer?

LORD Sir, it was I.

JAQUES Let's present him to the Duke like a Roman conqueror. And it would do well to set the deer's horns upon his head for a branch of victory. Have you no song, forester, for this purpose?

LORD Yes, sir.

JAQUES Sing it. 'Tis no matter how it be in tune, so it make noise enough.

Music

SONG

LORDS

10 What shall he have that killed the deer?
His leather skin and horns to wear.
Then sing him home, the rest shall bear
This burden.
Take thou no scorn to wear the horn,
It was a crest ere thou wast born,

Thy father's father wore it,
And thy father bore it,
The horn, the horn, the lusty horn,
Is not a thing to laugh to scorn. *Exeunt*

Enter Rosalind and Celia IV.3

ROSALIND How say you now? Is it not past two o'clock? And here much Orlando!

CELIA I warrant you, with pure love and troubled brain he hath ta'en his bow and arrows, and is gone forth to sleep.

Enter Silvius

Look who comes here.

SILVIUS
My errand is to you, fair youth:
My gentle Phebe did bid me give you this.

He gives Rosalind a letter, which she reads

I know not the contents, but as I guess
By the stern brow and waspish action 10
Which she did use as she was writing of it,
It bears an angry tenor. Pardon me,
I am but as a guiltless messenger.

ROSALIND
Patience herself would startle at this letter,
And play the swaggerer. Bear this, bear all.
She says I am not fair, that I lack manners,
She calls me proud, and that she could not love me
Were man as rare as phoenix. 'Od's my will,
Her love is not the hare that I do hunt!
Why writes she so to me? Well, shepherd, well, 20
This is a letter of your own device.

SILVIUS
No, I protest, I know not the contents;

Phebe did write it.

ROSALIND Come, come, you are a fool,
And turned into the extremity of love.
I saw her hand: she has a leathern hand,
A freestone-coloured hand; I verily did think
That her old gloves were on, but 'twas her hands;
She has a housewife's hand – but that's no matter.
I say she never did invent this letter;
30 This is a man's invention, and his hand.

SILVIUS
Sure, it is hers.

ROSALIND
Why, 'tis a boisterous and a cruel style,
A style for challengers. Why, she defies me,
Like Turk to Christian; women's gentle brain
Could not drop forth such giant rude invention,
Such Ethiop words, blacker in their effect
Than in their countenance. Will you hear the letter?

SILVIUS
So please you, for I never heard it yet;
Yet heard too much of Phebe's cruelty.

ROSALIND
40 She Phebes me; mark how the tyrant writes:
Art thou god to shepherd turned,
That a maiden's heart hath burned?
Can a woman rail thus?

SILVIUS Call you this railing?

ROSALIND
Why, thy godhead laid apart,
Warrest thou with a woman's heart?
Did you ever hear such railing?
Whiles the eye of man did woo me,
That could do no vengeance to me.
50 Meaning me a beast.

If the scorn of your bright eyne
Have power to raise such love in mine,
Alack, in me what strange effect
Would they work in mild aspect?
Whiles you chid me, I did love,
How then might your prayers move?
He that brings this love to thee
Little knows this love in me;
And by him seal up thy mind,
Whether that thy youth and kind 60
Will the faithful offer take
Of me and all that I can make,
Or else by him my love deny,
And then I'll study how to die.

SILVIUS Call you this chiding?

CELIA Alas, poor shepherd!

ROSALIND Do you pity him? No, he deserves no pity. – Wilt thou love such a woman? What, to make thee an instrument and play false strains upon thee? Not to be endured! Well, go your way to her – for I see love hath 70 made thee a tame snake – and say this to her: that if she love me, I charge her to love thee; if she will not, I will never have her, unless thou entreat for her. If you be a true lover, hence, and not a word, for here comes more company.

Exit Silvius

Enter Oliver

OLIVER
Good morrow, fair ones. Pray you, if you know,
Where in the purlieus of this forest stands
A sheepcote fenced about with olive trees?

CELIA
West of this place, down in the neighbour bottom,
The rank of osiers by the murmuring stream 80

Left on your right hand brings you to the place.
But at this hour the house doth keep itself,
There's none within.

OLIVER

If that an eye may profit by a tongue,
Then should I know you by description.
Such garments and such years: 'The boy is fair,
Of female favour, and bestows himself
Like a ripe sister; the woman low
And browner than her brother'. Are not you
90 The owner of the house I did inquire for?

CELIA

It is no boast, being asked, to say we are.

OLIVER

Orlando doth commend him to you both,
And to that youth he calls his 'Rosalind'
He sends this bloody napkin. Are you he?

ROSALIND

I am. What must we understand by this?

OLIVER

Some of my shame, if you will know of me
What man I am, and how, and why, and where
This handkercher was stained.

CELIA I pray you, tell it.

OLIVER

When last the young Orlando parted from you,
100 He left a promise to return again
Within an hour; and pacing through the forest,
Chewing the food of sweet and bitter fancy,
Lo, what befell! He threw his eye aside,
And mark what object did present itself!
Under an oak, whose boughs were mossed with age
And high top bald with dry antiquity,

A wretched ragged man, o'ergrown with hair,
Lay sleeping on his back. About his neck
A green and gilded snake had wreathed itself,
Who with her head nimble in threats approached 110
The opening of his mouth; but suddenly,
Seeing Orlando, it unlinked itself
And with indented glides did slip away
Into a bush: under which bush's shade
A lioness, with udders all drawn dry,
Lay couching, head on ground, with catlike watch
When that the sleeping man should stir; for 'tis
The royal disposition of that beast
To prey on nothing that doth seem as dead.
This seen, Orlando did approach the man, 120
And found it was his brother, his elder brother.

CELIA
O, I have heard him speak of that same brother,
And he did render him the most unnatural
That lived amongst men.

OLIVER And well he might so do,
For well I know he was unnatural.

ROSALIND
But to Orlando: did he leave him there,
Food to the sucked and hungry lioness?

OLIVER
Twice did he turn his back and purposed so.
But kindness, nobler ever than revenge,
And nature, stronger than his just occasion, 130
Made him give battle to the lioness,
Who quickly fell before him; in which hurtling
From miserable slumber I awaked.

CELIA
Are you his brother?

ROSALIND Was't you he rescued?

CELIA

Was't you that did so oft contrive to kill him?

OLIVER

'Twas I, but 'tis not I: I do not shame
To tell you what I was, since my conversion
So sweetly tastes, being the thing I am.

ROSALIND

But, for the bloody napkin?

OLIVER By and by.

140 When from the first to last betwixt us two
Tears our recountments had most kindly bathed,
As how I came into that desert place –
I'brief, he led me to the gentle Duke,
Who gave me fresh array and entertainment,
Committing me unto my brother's love,
Who led me instantly unto his cave,
There stripped himself, and here upon his arm
The lioness had torn some flesh away,
Which all this while had bled; and now he fainted,
150 And cried, in fainting, upon Rosalind.
Brief, I recovered him, bound up his wound,
And after some small space, being strong at heart,
He sent me hither, stranger as I am,
To tell this story, that you might excuse
His broken promise, and to give this napkin,
Dyed in this blood, unto the shepherd youth
That he in sport doth call his 'Rosalind'.

Rosalind faints

CELIA

Why, how now, Ganymede, sweet Ganymede!

OLIVER

Many will swoon when they do look on blood.

CELIA

160 There is more in it. – Cousin Ganymede!

OLIVER
Look, he recovers.

ROSALIND
I would I were at home.

CELIA We'll lead you thither. –
I pray you, will you take him by the arm?

OLIVER Be of good cheer, youth! You a man? You lack a man's heart.

ROSALIND I do so, I confess it. Ah, sirrah, a body would think this was well counterfeited. I pray you, tell your brother how well I counterfeited. Heigh-ho!

OLIVER This was not counterfeit, there is too great testimony in your complexion that it was a passion of earnest. 170

ROSALIND Counterfeit, I assure you.

OLIVER Well then, take a good heart, and counterfeit to be a man.

ROSALIND So I do; but, i'faith, I should have been a woman by right.

CELIA Come, you look paler and paler. Pray you, draw homewards. – Good sir, go with us.

OLIVER
That will I: for I must bear answer back
How you excuse my brother, Rosalind.

ROSALIND I shall devise something. But I pray you 180 commend my counterfeiting to him. Will you go?

Exeunt

*

Enter Touchstone and Audrey V.1

TOUCHSTONE We shall find a time, Audrey. Patience, gentle Audrey.

AUDREY Faith, the priest was good enough, for all the old gentleman's saying.

TOUCHSTONE A most wicked Sir Oliver, Audrey, a most vile Martext. But, Audrey, there is a youth here in the forest lays claim to you.

AUDREY Ay, I know who 'tis: he hath no interest in me in the world. Here comes the man you mean.

Enter William

10 TOUCHSTONE It is meat and drink to me to see a clown. By my troth, we that have good wits have much to answer for: we shall be flouting, we cannot hold.

WILLIAM Good even, Audrey.

AUDREY God ye good even, William.

WILLIAM And good even to you, sir.

TOUCHSTONE Good even, gentle friend. Cover thy head, cover thy head; nay, prithee, be covered. How old are you, friend?

WILLIAM Five-and-twenty, sir.

20 TOUCHSTONE A ripe age. Is thy name William?

WILLIAM William, sir.

TOUCHSTONE A fair name. Wast born i'th'forest here?

WILLIAM Ay, sir, I thank God.

TOUCHSTONE 'Thank God': a good answer. Art rich?

WILLIAM Faith, sir, so so.

TOUCHSTONE 'So so' is good, very good, very excellent good; and yet it is not, it is but so so. Art thou wise?

WILLIAM Ay, sir, I have a pretty wit.

TOUCHSTONE Why, thou sayest well. I do now remember
30 a saying: 'The fool doth think he is wise, but the wise man knows himself to be a fool'. The heathen philosopher, when he had a desire to eat a grape, would open his lips when he put it into his mouth, meaning thereby that grapes were made to eat and lips to open. You do love this maid?

WILLIAM I do, sir.

TOUCHSTONE Give me your hand. Art thou learned?

WILLIAM No, sir.

TOUCHSTONE Then learn this of me. To have is to have. For it is a figure in rhetoric that drink, being poured out 40 of a cup into a glass, by filling the one doth empty the other; for all your writers do consent that 'ipse' is he. Now, you are not 'ipse', for I am he.

WILLIAM Which he, sir?

TOUCHSTONE He, sir, that must marry this woman. Therefore, you clown, abandon – which is in the vulgar 'leave' – the society – which in the boorish is 'company' – of this female – which in the common is 'woman' – which, together, is 'abandon the society of this female', or, clown, thou perishest; or, to thy better understand- 50 ing, diest; or, to wit, I kill thee, make thee away, translate thy life into death, thy liberty into bondage. I will deal in poison with thee, or in bastinado, or in steel; I will bandy with thee in faction; I will o'er-run thee with policy; I will kill thee a hundred and fifty ways – therefore tremble and depart.

AUDREY Do, good William.

WILLIAM God rest you merry, sir. *Exit*

Enter Corin

CORIN Our master and mistress seeks you: come away, away. 60

TOUCHSTONE Trip, Audrey, trip, Audrey. I attend, I attend. *Exeunt*

Enter Orlando and Oliver V.2

ORLANDO Is't possible, that on so little acquaintance you should like her? That, but seeing, you should love her? And loving woo? And, wooing, she should grant? And will you persever to enjoy her?

OLIVER Neither call the giddiness of it in question: the

poverty of her, the small acquaintance, my sudden wooing, nor her sudden consenting; but say with me 'I love Aliena'; say with her that she loves me; consent with both that we may enjoy each other. It shall be to
10 your good, for my father's house and all the revenue that was old Sir Rowland's will I estate upon you, and here live and die a shepherd.

Enter Rosalind

ORLANDO You have my consent. Let your wedding be tomorrow. Thither will I invite the Duke and all's contented followers. Go you and prepare Aliena; for, look you, here comes my Rosalind.

ROSALIND God save you, brother.

OLIVER And you, fair sister. *Exit*

ROSALIND O my dear Orlando, how it grieves me to see
20 thee wear thy heart in a scarf.

ORLANDO It is my arm.

ROSALIND I thought thy heart had been wounded with the claws of a lion.

ORLANDO Wounded it is, but with the eyes of a lady.

ROSALIND Did your brother tell you how I counterfeited to sound, when he showed me your handkercher?

ORLANDO Ay, and greater wonders than that.

ROSALIND O, I know where you are. Nay, 'tis true; there was never anything so sudden but the fight of two rams,
30 and Caesar's thrasonical brag of 'I came, saw, and overcame'. For your brother and my sister no sooner met but they looked; no sooner looked but they loved; no sooner loved but they sighed; no sooner sighed but they asked one another the reason; no sooner knew the reason but they sought the remedy: and in these degrees have they made a pair of stairs to marriage which they will climb incontinent or else be incontinent before marriage. They are in the very wrath of love and

they will together; clubs cannot part them.

ORLANDO They shall be married tomorrow; and I will 40 bid the Duke to the nuptial. But, O, how bitter a thing it is to look into happiness through another man's eyes! By so much the more shall I tomorrow be at the height of heart-heaviness, by how much I shall think my brother happy in having what he wishes for.

ROSALIND Why, then, tomorrow I cannot serve your turn for Rosalind?

ORLANDO I can live no longer by thinking.

ROSALIND I will weary you then no longer with idle talking. Know of me then, for now I speak to some 50 purpose, that I know you are a gentleman of good conceit. I speak not this that you should bear a good opinion of my knowledge, insomuch I say I know you are; neither do I labour for a greater esteem than may in some little measure draw a belief from you to do yourself good, and not to grace me. Believe then, if you please, that I can do strange things: I have, since I was three year old, conversed with a magician, most profound in his art, and yet not damnable. If you do love Rosalind so near the heart as your gesture cries it out, 60 when your brother marries Aliena, shall you marry her. I know into what straits of fortune she is driven, and it is not impossible to me, if it appear not inconvenient to you, to set her before your eyes tomorrow, human as she is, and without any danger.

ORLANDO Speakest thou in sober meanings?

ROSALIND By my life I do, which I tender dearly though I say I am a magician. Therefore, put you in your best array, bid your friends; for if you will be married tomorrow, you shall; and to Rosalind, if you will. 70

Enter Silvius and Phebe

Look, here comes a lover of mine and a lover of hers.

PHEBE

Youth, you have done me much ungentleness,
To show the letter that I writ to you.

ROSALIND

I care not if I have: it is my study
To seem despiteful and ungentle to you.
You are there followed by a faithful shepherd;
Look upon him, love him: he worships you.

PHEBE

Good shepherd, tell this youth what 'tis to love.

SILVIUS

It is to be all made of sighs and tears,
80 And so am I for Phebe.

PHEBE

And I for Ganymede.

ORLANDO

And I for Rosalind.

ROSALIND

And I for no woman.

SILVIUS

It is to be all made of faith and service,
And so am I for Phebe.

PHEBE

And I for Ganymede.

ORLANDO

And I for Rosalind.

ROSALIND

And I for no woman.

SILVIUS

It is to be all made of fantasy,
90 All made of passion, and all made of wishes,
All adoration, duty and observance,
All humbleness, all patience, and impatience,
All purity, all trial, all observance;

And so am I for Phebe.

PHEBE

And so am I for Ganymede.

ORLANDO

And so am I for Rosalind.

ROSALIND

And so am I for no woman.

PHEBE (*to Rosalind*)

If this be so, why blame you me to love you?

SILVIUS (*to Phebe*)

If this be so, why blame you me to love you?

ORLANDO

If this be so, why blame you me to love you? 100

ROSALIND Why do you speak too 'Why blame you me to love you?'

ORLANDO

To her that is not here, nor doth not hear.

ROSALIND Pray you no more of this, 'tis like the howling of Irish wolves against the moon. (*To Silvius*) I will help you, if I can. (*To Phebe*) I would love you, if I could. – Tomorrow meet me all together. (*To Phebe*) I will marry you if ever I marry woman, and I'll be married tomorrow. (*To Orlando*) I will satisfy you, if ever I satisfied man, and you shall be married tomorrow. 110 (*To Silvius*) I will content you, if what pleases you contents you, and you shall be married tomorrow. (*To Orlando*) As you love Rosalind, meet. (*To Silvius*) As you love Phebe, meet. – And as I love no woman, I'll meet. So, fare you well; I have left you commands.

SILVIUS I'll not fail, if I live.

PHEBE Nor I.

ORLANDO Nor I. *Exeunt*

V.3 *Enter Touchstone and Audrey*

TOUCHSTONE Tomorrow is the joyful day, Audrey. Tomorrow will we be married.

AUDREY I do desire it with all my heart; and I hope it is no dishonest desire to desire to be a woman of the world? Here come two of the banished Duke's pages.

Enter two Pages

FIRST PAGE Well met, honest gentleman.

TOUCHSTONE By my troth, well met. Come, sit, sit, and a song.

SECOND PAGE We are for you. Sit i'th'middle.

10 FIRST PAGE Shall we clap into't roundly, without hawking, or spitting, or saying we are hoarse, which are the only prologues to a bad voice?

SECOND PAGE I'faith, i'faith; and both in a tune, like two gypsies on a horse.

SONG

PAGES

It was a lover and his lass,
  With a hey, and a ho, and a hey nonino,
That o'er the green corn field did pass,
  In the spring time, the only pretty ring time,
When birds do sing, hey ding a ding, ding,
20 Sweet lovers love the spring.

Between the acres of the rye,
  With a hey, and a ho, and a hey nonino,
These pretty country folks would lie,
  In spring time, the only pretty ring time,
When birds do sing, hey ding a ding, ding,
Sweet lovers love the spring.

This carol they began that hour,
  With a hey, and a ho, and a hey nonino,

How that a life was but a flower,
In spring time, the only pretty ring time, 30
When birds do sing, hey ding a ding, ding,
Sweet lovers love the spring.

And therefore take the present time,
With a hey, and a ho, and a hey nonino,
For love is crownèd with the prime,
In spring time, the only pretty ring time,
When birds do sing, hey ding a ding, ding,
Sweet lovers love the spring.

TOUCHSTONE Truly, young gentlemen, though there was no great matter in the ditty, yet the note was very 40 untuneable.

FIRST PAGE You are deceived, sir; we kept time, we lost not our time.

TOUCHSTONE By my troth, yes: I count it but time lost to hear such a foolish song. God buy you, and God mend your voices! Come, Audrey. *Exeunt*

Enter Duke Senior, Amiens, Jaques, Orlando, Oliver, and Celia V.4

DUKE
Dost thou believe, Orlando, that the boy
Can do all this that he hath promised?

ORLANDO
I sometimes do believe, and sometimes do not,
As those that fear they hope, and know they fear.
Enter Rosalind, Silvius, and Phebe

ROSALIND
Patience once more, whiles our compact is urged.
(*to the Duke*) You say, if I bring in your Rosalind,
You will bestow her on Orlando here?

DUKE

That would I, had I kingdoms to give with her.

ROSALIND (*to Orlando*)

And you say you will have her, when I bring her?

ORLANDO

10 That would I, were I of all kingdoms king.

ROSALIND (*to Phebe*)

You say you'll marry me, if I be willing?

PHEBE

That will I, should I die the hour after.

ROSALIND

But if you do refuse to marry me,
You'll give yourself to this most faithful shepherd?

PHEBE

So is the bargain.

ROSALIND (*to Silvius*)

You say that you'll have Phebe, if she will?

SILVIUS

Though to have her and death were both one thing.

ROSALIND

I have promised to make all this matter even.
Keep you your word, O Duke, to give your daughter;
20 You yours, Orlando, to receive his daughter;
Keep you your word, Phebe, that you'll marry me
Or else, refusing me, to wed this shepherd;
Keep your word, Silvius, that you'll marry her,
If she refuse me – and from hence I go,
To make these doubts all even.

Exeunt Rosalind and Celia

DUKE

I do remember in this shepherd boy
Some lively touches of my daughter's favour.

ORLANDO

My lord, the first time that I ever saw him

Methought he was a brother to your daughter.
But, my good lord, this boy is forest-born, 30
And hath been tutored in the rudiments
Of many desperate studies by his uncle,
Whom he reports to be a great magician,

Enter Touchstone and Audrey

Obscurèd in the circle of this forest.

JAQUES There is sure another flood toward, and these couples are coming to the ark. Here comes a pair of very strange beasts, which in all tongues are called fools.

TOUCHSTONE Salutation and greeting to you all!

JAQUES Good my lord, bid him welcome: this is the motley-minded gentleman that I have so often met in 40 the forest. He hath been a courtier, he swears.

TOUCHSTONE If any man doubt that, let him put me to my purgation. I have trod a measure, I have flattered a lady, I have been politic with my friend, smooth with mine enemy, I have undone three tailors, I have had four quarrels, and like to have fought one.

JAQUES And how was that ta'en up?

TOUCHSTONE Faith, we met, and found the quarrel was upon the seventh cause.

JAQUES How seventh cause? – Good my lord, like this 50 fellow.

DUKE I like him very well.

TOUCHSTONE God 'ild you, sir, I desire you of the like. I press in here, sir, amongst the rest of the country copulatives, to swear and to forswear, according as marriage binds and blood breaks. A poor virgin, sir, an ill-favoured thing, sir, but mine own, a poor humour of mine, sir, to take that that no man else will. Rich honesty dwells like a miser, sir, in a poor house, as your pearl in your foul oyster. 60

DUKE By my faith, he is very swift and sententious.

TOUCHSTONE According to the fool's bolt, sir, and such dulcet diseases.

JAQUES But for the seventh cause. How did you find the quarrel on the seventh cause?

TOUCHSTONE Upon a lie seven times removed. – Bear your body more seeming, Audrey. – As thus, sir. I did dislike the cut of a certain courtier's beard. He sent me word, if I said his beard was not cut well, he was in the
70 mind it was: this is called the Retort Courteous. If I sent him word again it was not well cut, he would send me word he cut it to please himself: this is called the Quip Modest. If again 'it was not well cut', he disabled my judgement: this is called the Reply Churlish. If again 'it was not well cut', he would answer, I spake not true: this is called the Reproof Valiant. If again 'it was not well cut', he would say, I lie: this is called the Countercheck Quarrelsome: and so to Lie Circumstantial and the Lie Direct.

80 JAQUES And how oft did you say his beard was not well cut?

TOUCHSTONE I durst go no further than the Lie Circumstantial, nor he durst not give me the Lie Direct. And so we measured swords and parted.

JAQUES Can you nominate in order now the degrees of the lie?

TOUCHSTONE O sir, we quarrel in print, by the book, as you have books for good manners. I will name you the degrees. The first, the Retort Courteous; the second,
90 the Quip Modest; the third, the Reply Churlish; the fourth, the Reproof Valiant; the fifth, the Countercheck Quarrelsome; the sixth, the Lie with Circumstance; the seventh, the Lie Direct. All these you may avoid but the Lie Direct; and you may avoid that too, with an 'If'. I knew when seven justices could not take

up a quarrel, but when the parties were met themselves, one of them thought but of an 'If': as, 'If you said so, then I said so'; and they shook hands and swore brothers. Your 'If' is the only peace-maker; much virtue in 'If'. 100

JAQUES Is not this a rare fellow, my lord? He's as good at anything, and yet a fool.

DUKE He uses his folly like a stalking-horse, and under the presentation of that he shoots his wit.

Enter a masquer representing Hymen, and Rosalind and Celia as themselves. Still music

HYMEN

Then is there mirth in heaven,
When earthly things, made even,
Atone together.
Good Duke, receive thy daughter,
Hymen from heaven brought her,
Yea, brought her hither 110
That thou mightst join her hand with his
Whose heart within her bosom is.

ROSALIND (*to the Duke*)

To you I give myself, for I am yours.
(*to Orlando*)
To you I give myself, for I am yours.

DUKE

If there be truth in sight, you are my daughter.

ORLANDO

If there be truth in sight, you are my Rosalind.

PHEBE

If sight and shape be true,
Why then, my love adieu!

ROSALIND (*to the Duke*)

I'll have no father, if you be not he;
(*to Orlando*)

120 I'll have no husband, if you be not he;
(*to Phebe*)
Nor ne'er wed woman, if you be not she.

HYMEN

Peace, ho! I bar confusion.
'Tis I must make conclusion
  Of these most strange events.
Here's eight that must take hands,
To join in Hymen's bands,
  If truth holds true contents.
(*to Orlando and Rosalind*)
You and you no cross shall part;
(*to Oliver and Celia*)
You and you are heart in heart;
(*to Phebe*)
130 You to his love must accord,
Or have a woman to your lord;
(*to Touchstone and Audrey*)
You and you are sure together,
As the winter to foul weather.
Whiles a wedlock-hymn we sing,
Feed yourselves with questioning,
That reason wonder may diminish
How thus we met, and these things finish.

SONG

Wedding is great Juno's crown,
  O blessèd bond of board and bed;
140 'Tis Hymen peoples every town,
  High wedlock then be honourèd;
Honour, high honour and renown
To Hymen, god of every town!

DUKE

O my dear niece, welcome thou art to me,
Even daughter, welcome, in no less degree.

PHEBE (*to Silvius*)
I will not eat my word, now thou art mine,
Thy faith my fancy to thee doth combine.
Enter Second Brother, Jaques de Boys

JAQUES DE BOYS
Let me have audience for a word or two.
I am the second son of old Sir Rowland
That bring these tidings to this fair assembly. 150
Duke Frederick, hearing how that every day
Men of great worth resorted to this forest,
Addressed a mighty power, which were on foot,
In his own conduct, purposely to take
His brother here and put him to the sword;
And to the skirts of this wild wood he came,
Where, meeting with an old religious man,
After some question with him, was converted
Both from his enterprise and from the world,
His crown bequeathing to his banished brother, 160
And all their lands restored to them again
That were with him exiled. This to be true,
I do engage my life.

DUKE Welcome, young man.
Thou offerest fairly to thy brothers' wedding:
To one his lands withheld, and to the other
A land itself at large, a potent dukedom.
First, in this forest, let us do those ends
That here were well begun and well begot;
And after, every of this happy number
That have endured shrewd days and nights with us 170
Shall share the good of our returnèd fortune
According to the measure of their states.
Meantime, forget this new-fallen dignity,
And fall into our rustic revelry:
Play, music, and you brides and bridegrooms all,

With measure heaped in joy, to th'measures fall.

JAQUES

Sir, by your patience. – If I heard you rightly,
The Duke hath put on a religious life,
And thrown into neglect the pompous court?

JAQUES DE BOYS

180 He hath.

JAQUES

To him will I: out of these convertites
There is much matter to be heard and learned.
(*to the Duke*)
You to your former honour I bequeath:
Your patience and your virtue well deserves it;
(*to Orlando*)
You to a love that your true faith doth merit;
(*to Oliver*)
You to your land, and love, and great allies;
(*to Silvius*)
You to a long and well deservèd bed;
(*to Touchstone*)
And you to wrangling, for thy loving voyage
Is but for two months victualled. – So to your
pleasures:
190 I am for other than for dancing measures.

DUKE

Stay, Jaques, stay.

JAQUES

To see no pastime, I. What you would have
I'll stay to know at your abandoned cave. *Exit*

DUKE

Proceed, proceed. We'll begin these rites
As we do trust they'll end, in true delights.

Exeunt all except Rosalind

ROSALIND It is not the fashion to see the lady the epilogue, but it is no more unhandsome than to see the lord the prologue. If it be true that good wine needs no bush, 'tis true that a good play needs no epilogue. Yet to good wine they do use good bushes, and good plays prove 200 the better by the help of good epilogues. What a case am I in, then, that am neither a good epilogue nor cannot insinuate with you in the behalf of a good play? I am not furnished like a beggar; therefore to beg will not become me. My way is to conjure you, and I'll begin with the women. I charge you, O women, for the love you bear to men, to like as much of this play as please you; and I charge you, O men, for the love you bear to women – as I perceive by your simpering, none of you hates them – that between you and the women the play 210 may please. If I were a woman, I would kiss as many of you as had beards that pleased me, complexions that liked me, and breaths that I defied not; and, I am sure, as many as have good beards, or good faces, or sweet breaths, will, for my kind offer, when I make curtsy, bid me farewell. *Exit*

COMMENTARY

IN the following pages no attempt has been made to 'explain' characteristics of Elizabethan syntax that present no difficulties in comprehension. Accordingly there are no separate notes on, for example, the so-called third-person plural in '-s' (*the Destinies decrees*), the 'attraction' of the verb to the nearer subject (*thou and I am*), the double negatives, the subjunctives, or such constructions as *better than him I am before knows me*. These are all described in E. A. Abbott's *A Shakespearian Grammar*, which, even if in some ways old-fashioned (it was first published in 1869), is still extremely helpful; and in G. L. Brook, *The Language of Shakespeare* (London, 1976).

Throughout the Commentary and the Account of the Text, the abbreviation 'F' is used for the First Folio of 1623, in which the play was first published. References in the Introduction and Commentary to other plays by Shakespeare not yet available in the New Penguin Shakespeare edition are to Peter Alexander's edition of the Complete Works (London, 1951).

The Characters in the Play

This list is not in F. For comment on the naming of the two Dukes and on the two characters named Jaques, see Introduction, pages 40 and 41–2. That *Jaques* was almost certainly two syllables (pronounced 'Jak-es' or, more probably, 'Jake-wes', in either case with a pun on 'jakes') is suggested by lines like 'The melancholy Jaques grieves at that' or (from Robert Greene's *Friar Bacon and Friar Bungay*) 'Whose surname is Don Jaques Vandermast' and 'Bestir thee, Jaques, tak e not now the foil'. Jaques was also an English family name, as was de Boys.

As You Like It is one of the few Shakespeare texts fully divided in the original editions into Acts and Scenes (the formula used in F being '*Actus primus. Scæna Prima*' etc.). Since it is improbable that such divisions were observed on the Elizabethan public stage where, except perhaps for one interval, the action seems to have been continuous, the text of this play may have been specially prepared for publication.

I.1.2 ***but poor a thousand*** a mere (or, in modern idiom, a 'miserable') thousand. Compare *a many* in line 109.

3 ***charged*** it was charged, order was given to

on his blessing as a condition of obtaining, or retaining, his (our father's) blessing

4 ***breed*** raise, educate

5 ***school*** (probably) university

6 ***his profit*** his progress, the way in which he benefits

7 ***stays*** retains (or 'detains')

11 ***fair with*** healthy as a result of

manage. This was the technical term for the training of a horse in its paces, particularly for military purposes (from French *manège*, itself now used as an English word).

16 ***countenance*** demeanour, bearing; or style of living (as allowed to Orlando)

17 ***hinds*** servants, farm labourers

bars me excludes me from

18–19 ***as much as in him lies, mines my gentility with my education*** to the best of his ability undermines the advantages I have from my gentle birth, by the poor kind of education he allows me

26 ***shake me up*** abuse me violently

27 ***make*** do (but Orlando's reply involves a pun on the word)

30 ***Marry*** by Mary (with a pun on *mar*, just used by Oliver)

33–4 ***be naught a while*** leave me, 'make yourself scarce', or (possibly) be quiet

36 *prodigal portion* (with reference to the parable of the prodigal son, Luke 15.11 ff., and particularly 15–17)

39 *orchard.* The commonest Elizabethan meaning was 'garden', although sometimes the distinction was drawn between orchard and garden.

42–3 *in the gentle condition of blood* if your behaviour was what that of a brother, of gentle blood, should be

48 *nearer to his reverence* more worthy of the respect due to him (the father), because as eldest son 'closest' to him in blood. Oliver's anger is more convincingly explained by Orlando's tone than by anything in the single phrase.

49, 50 (stage directions) *threatening him*; *seizing him by the throat.* These are not in F, but the action is made clear by lines 56–7.

49 *boy.* The word is suggested by Orlando's being younger but was a general term of contempt. Compare Coriolanus's anger when it is used of him, V.6.101–17, and *Romeo and Juliet*, III.1.65 and 130.

51 *young* inexperienced, immature. Perhaps there is also a pun on *elder* in the previous line: the elder tree, associated with Judas, may have had connotations of unreliability and deceit.

52 *villain.* Orlando chooses to take the word in its other sense of 'serf' (our 'villein'). His and Oliver's use for the first time of the contemptuous second-person singular indicates that the quarrel has become ill-tempered. On its use elsewhere in the play, see Introduction, page 33.

65 *qualities.* In addition to its modern senses, the word could mean 'accomplishments', 'occupations', 'ranks'.

67 *exercises* employments, occupations

68 *allottery* allocation, share

72 *will* (1) desire; (2) portion from the will or testament

80 *grow upon me* (probably another quibble) grow up too fast for my liking; take liberties with me; grow rank (hence *rankness* in line 81)

81 *physic* cure (by a dose of physic), correct

91 *new news*. See Introduction, page 39.

103-4 *to stay* if forced to stay

111-12 *fleet the time carelessly as they did in the golden world* while away the time in a carefree way as men did in the Golden Age. *Fleet* is normally an intransitive verb, meaning to 'float', 'pass quickly' or 'glide away'; Shakespeare perhaps invents this use of it to mean 'cause to pass quickly'.

120 *shall* must, will need to

121 *tender* undeveloped

122 *foil*. This may mean only 'defeat', but the noun was also a technical term used in wrestling for a successful throwing of the opponent that yet did not result in a formal 'fall'. *Foil* is used again thus at II.2.14.

124 *withal* with it

125 *brook* endure

131 *underhand* secret, unobtrusive. The derogatory implication was not yet inevitable. (Compare *natural* in line 135.)

134 *an envious emulator of* one who hates and is jealous of

139 *grace himself on thee* gain honour at your expense by defeating you

practise plot

145 *anatomize* dissect (in the surgical sense, and so it came to mean 'analyse' and 'reveal')

149-50 *go alone* walk without a support (he will be crippled and will need a crutch)

153 *gamester* athlete (but often with derogatory, sometimes with favourable, connotations - like Synge's, and indeed the frequent Irish, use of 'playboy')

156 *device*. Perhaps this means here 'aspiration' rather than 'invention' or 'manner of thinking'.

sorts classes

enchantingly as if by a real process of enchanting or bewitching

159 *misprized* despised or (possibly) underrated

160 *clear all* solve all problems

I.2.1 *coz.* An abbreviation of 'cousin' (which itself could be used of any relative, as the Duke later in I.3.40 uses it to Rosalind) but here and throughout the play probably used rather as a term of affection than strictly of the blood relationship of Rosalind and Celia.

3 *would you yet were.* The emendation to 'would you yet I were' turns the phrase into a question 'do you want me to be even merrier than that?'; the F text, preserved here, means 'I wish you at least were merrier, whatever be my feelings'.

5 *learn* teach (not then only a dialectal or 'incorrect' use)

9 *so* provided that

12 *righteously tempered* correctly compounded, blended (an unusual sense of 'righteous')

16 *nor none.* Double negative is common in Shakespeare and does not even necessarily imply emphatic statement. Compare line 26.

18–19 *perforce* forcibly

19 *render* give back to

27–8 *than with safety of a pure blush thou mayst in honour come off again* than will enable you to come out of the affair (or escape) with your honour safe and at no more expense than a pure blush (not the blush of shame)

30 *housewife.* This is used here as a half-derogatory term: the goddess Fortune, turning her wheel (the symbol of chance, inconstancy), is compared with a mere housewife, spinning. Compare 'Dame Fortune'.

37 *honest* chaste

39–40 *Fortune's office to Nature's.* Some commentators place great stress on this conventional contrast between Nature (responsible for beauty and such lasting gifts as intelligence or *wit*) and Fortune (responsible for wealth and position, which can easily be changed), and elevate it into the major 'theme' of the play; the usurper's court is even equated with Fortune, the Forest of Arden with Nature. Shakespeare has other, subtler, things to say.

41 (stage direction) *Enter Touchstone.* The F stage direction is '*Enter Clowne*', and Shakespeare may have intended 'Touchstone' to be only the name that the clown adopts in the Forest. See Introduction, page 16, and note on line 53 below.

44 *flout* mock

47 *Nature's natural* one who by nature is deficient in intelligence: the 'natural' as opposed to the professional fool. Touchstone, however, immediately assumes the role of the latter (see Introduction, page 16) and Celia is presumably jesting at his expense.

52 *whetstone.* Although the whetstone (for sharpening tools) is not the same as a touchstone (for testing metals), the jest has more point if Celia (or Shakespeare) already thinks of Touchstone as the clown's name.

53–4 *How now, wit, whither wander you?* 'Wit, whither wilt?' was proverbial, addressed to one who was romancing; and there is a further pun on the 'wandering' of the clown's 'wit'.

57 *messenger* (used not only of one bringing a message but also of the official employed to arrest a state prisoner)

62 *pancakes* meat-cakes, fritters

63 *naught* worthless

stand to it swear to it, justify the statement that. Of these passages of wit, Shaw complained 'Who would endure such humor from any one but Shakespeare? – an Eskimo would demand his money back if a modern author offered him such fare'.

79–81 *My father's love . . . these days.* F gives these lines to Rosalind. For comment, see Introduction, page 40. The F compositor who set these lines (Compositor 'B') made similar errors with other speech prefixes in V.1 (on R6^{v} of F), but they were discovered during proof-reading and corrected; and another of the compositors ('D') made similar errors in II.3 (on Q5^{v}) that were not corrected until the Second Folio years later. See also the Account of the Text, pages 191–2.

80 *taxation* criticism, satire. The theory that a secondary meaning is involved, because the Latin 'tax' means 'the sound of a whip stroke', is not fully convincing.

84–6 *since the little wit . . . a great show.* For the possible topical allusion, see Introduction, pages 37–8.

87 *the Beu.* The F reading is preserved here (most editors emend to 'Le Beau') on the assumption that Celia is mocking Le Beau and his mincing speech. (The F spelling '*Boon-iour*' in line 93 perhaps has the same intention.) Only in the following stage direction, however, is the name ever spelt '*Beau*' in F; elsewhere it is '*Beu*'.

89 *put on us* force on us, ram down our throats. Possibly Celia purses her lips in mimicry of Le Beau to make the point clearer.

92 *the more marketable* more easily sold, at a profit, because our weights will have been increased

95 *colour* type, kind (a normal Elizabethan meaning, but Le Beau's reply perhaps suggests that he is incapable of understanding it)

98 *Or as the Destinies decrees.* Touchstone, here and in line 100, is also aping Le Beau and is deliberately pompous: hence Celia's reply.

100 *rank.* The *adjective* can mean 'offensively strong in smell', a meaning that Rosalind seizes on.

102 *amaze* bewilder

106–7 *yet to do* still to come

109 *Well, the beginning that is dead and buried.* This has often been taken as a question but may be a cynical comment on Le Beau's obvious delight in making much of what is already past.

112 *proper* handsome

114 *bills* notices, proclamations (such as are sometimes carried on the back, slung from the neck). Conceivably there is a pun on *bills* meaning 'halberds'. Le Beau's over-formal language reminds Rosalind of legal jargon and she replies with a legal phrase and a pun on *presence* ('presents', legal documents).

118 *that* so that

121 *dole* lamentation

131–2 *broken music*. The usual meaning, 'part music', hardly makes sense here. The gloss 'broken instruments' (with broken ribs or frets) is better than this (or than 'broken consort').

138 (stage direction) *Flourish* a fanfare of horns or trumpets (normally to mark the entrance of a king, queen, or other ruler)

140 *forwardness* rashness

148 *such odds in the man* so marked a superiority in the man (Charles), so much in the man's favour (as against the youth)

163 *with your eyes* clearly, as you really are

168–9 *therefore be misprized* be condemned, or undervalued, on that account

172 *wherein* in a matter in which

175 *gracious* graced, lucky enough to enjoy favour (including the favours of Fortune)

184 *deceived* mistaken (through underestimating your strength)

190 *working* aim

196 *come your ways* come on

197 *be thy speed* speed thee, grant thee success

205 *breathed* exercised. The modern idiom is 'have not yet warmed up'.

214 *still* always

220–22 *I am more proud to be Sir Rowland's son, | . . . to Frederick*. Perhaps these words are spoken, in defiance, as the Duke leaves the stage.

221 *calling* station in life (rather than 'title', a meaning for which there is no recorded authority)

230 *Sticks me at heart* pierces (me in) my heart

232 *justly* precisely

233 (stage direction) *taking a chain from her neck*. The warrant for this addition to F is III.2.175.

234 *out of suits with* dismissed from the favour of (and

therefore, like a dismissed servant, deprived of the *suit* or livery)

240 *quintain* the post, block, or perhaps figure used for tilting practice

242 *would* wishes

245 *Have with you* I am coming with you

247 *urged conference* invited conversation

249 *Or* either

253 *condition* temper or mood

254 *misconsters* misconstrues (a variant form, with the accent on the second syllable)

255 *humorous* the victim of a disproportion of the four 'humours' (which had to be in perfect balance in a man's make-up if he was to be normal)

261 *taller*. For the complete contradiction between this and all other references to Rosalind's height, and Celia's, see Introduction, pages 40–41.

264 *whose*. The general sense, not any particular word, provides the antecedent for *whose*, which refers to both the daughters just mentioned.

268 *argument* line of reasoning

273 *in a better world than this* if we should meet in happier circumstances

275 *bounden* indebted

276 *smother* the dense and more suffocating smoke of the smouldering fire. The corresponding modern idiom is 'out of the frying pan into the fire'.

278 *Rosalind*. Here, and in the first stage direction and the text of I.3, F has *Rosaline*. It is often difficult in Elizabethan ('secretary') handwriting to distinguish between *e* and *d*; but 'Rosaline' and 'Rosalind' may only be alternative forms of the one name. Rosaline is the heroine of *Love's Labour's Lost*, and Romeo's first love was Rosaline. The verses of Orlando and Touchstone in III.2 show that 'Rosalind' is the heroine's 'real' name here – though pronounced, or jocularly mispronounced, to rhyme with 'lined'.

I.3.11 *child's father*. For the defence of this F reading, see Introduction, pages 24–6.

14 *trodden paths*. Perhaps Celia is implying that she and Rosalind were unconventional in speaking as they did to Orlando after the wrestling.

18 *Hem*. This is a pun on the two senses, the one from sewing, the other imitating the sound of a cough; it is suggested by *burs* ('bur' could also refer to a choking sensation in the throat).

19–20 *cry 'hem' and have him*. This time the pun is on *hem* and *him*. Some commentators have thought the phrase proverbial but it is not listed in the usual source books.

24 *try* try a bout or wrestling match (with Orlando – with the usual sexual pun on *fall*)

31 *chase* pursuit, sequence (another pun, from hunting)

32 *dearly* intensely

39 *your safest haste* all speed possible, in the interests of your own safety

40 *cousin* niece

47 *frantic* out of my senses

51 *purgation*. In addition to the medical meaning, the word was used in theology (both of the purification of the soul in Purgatory and of the declaration of innocence on oath) and as a legal term, of the proving of innocence, particularly by ordeal. Compare V.4.42–3.

60 *friends* (apparently used in the now obsolete sense, 'relatives')

61 *What's that to me?* How is that relevant to me?

65 *stayed* retained, kept

68 *remorse*. The word already had its modern meaning of 'compunction' or 'repentance', but also commonly meant 'compassion'.

69 *too young*. For comment on the time-scheme, see Introduction, page 39.

71 *still* always, constantly

73 *Juno's swans*. The author of the anonymous play *Soliman and Perseda* (possibly Kyd) also refers to

'Juno's goodly swans | Or Venus' milk-white doves', although most Elizabethans knew and accepted the classical tradition that the swans were Venus's birds (Juno's being peacocks). The 'explanation' that Shakespeare is transferring the symbolic qualities of Venus, goddess of love, to Juno, goddess of marriage (and 'patroness' of this play), seems strained and somewhat desperate.

81 *doom* judgement, sentence

102 *now at our sorrows pale* now pale or overcast in sympathy with our sorrows

110 *umber* yellow-coloured earth (so named from Umbria, in Italy). The point is that Elizabethan ladies of degree took care to protect their complexions from the sun, and their paleness would have been in marked contrast to the complexions of country women.

111 *pass along* go on our way

113 *more than common tall.* This contradicts I.2.261, which is almost certainly 'wrong'. See Introduction, pages 40–41.

114 *suit me all points* dress and equip myself in all ways

115 *curtle-axe* short sword. This form of the noun 'coutelas' (our 'cutlass') arose by mistaken etymology.

118 *swashing* swaggering. The word (or its variant 'washing') was used also of a blow in fencing, as in *Romeo and Juliet*, I.1.61–2: *Gregory, remember thy washing blow.*

outside. Perhaps, but not necessarily, in the tailoring sense (as contrasted with the lining). Similarly, *outface* in line 120 perhaps contains a pun on the tailoring sense of 'face', meaning 'trim'.

119 *mannish* masculine

120 *outface it with their semblances* bluff it out (the 'indefinite *it*'), relying on their mere appearance of strength

126 *Aliena* the stranger, or one who is 'not herself'. The accentuation is in doubt, but a stress on the second syllable seems possible in this line.

127 *assayed* attempted

131 *woo* win over, persuade

II.1 (stage direction) *like foresters* (probably) in 'Kentish green'

4 *envious* given to enmity or hatred

5 *the penalty of Adam.* According to the traditional view, in Eden there was perpetual spring; the change of seasons, with the hardships of winter, was a consequence of Adam's fall. Apparently, the Duke asks a third question, 'Do we not feel?', and goes on to imply that it is nevertheless a good thing so to feel, for the reasons he gives.

11 *feelingly* by making themselves felt

12 *uses of* (perhaps both 'ways of life associated with' and 'profits to be had from')

13–14 *the toad ... | ... head.* Two superstitions of natural history are alluded to here: that the toad was poisonous and that it had a precious stone (alternatively, a bone) in its head that had magical properties and was an antidote against poison.

15 *exempt from public haunt* not exposed to, or visited by, people generally

18 *I would not change it.* Some editors unnecessarily transfer these words to the Duke. As Furness said, 'The Duke has asked a question. Is no one to answer?'

22 *fools.* This means 'simple creatures', not 'idiots'. Compare line 40.

23 *burghers* citizens, of the woods, their own territories (*confines*)

24 *forkèd heads* barbed arrows

27 *kind* respect

31 *antick.* Possibly only 'old' (our 'antique'), but possibly 'antic' in the sense of 'contorted', 'queerly shaped'. The word is to be stressed on the first syllable.

33 *sequestered* separated

41 *of* by

44 *moralize* draw morals from, or explicate

46 *needless* unneeding (the stream had water enough already)

50 *of* by

velvet friend. Velvet must refer to the coat of the deer, although it is also the technical term for the covering of the developing horns of a stag; *friend* has been altered by some editors to 'friends'. In any case, it is the deer that is abandoned, not Jaques; the pronouns create some confusion throughout this speech.

51–2 *part | The flux* separate (or 'separate the miserable one *from*') the flood. The phrase may be basically proverbial.

52 *careless* carefree

58 *invectively* vehemently

61 *and what's worse* and everything that is even worse

67 *cope* encounter and engage with (in combat or debate)

I.2.3 *Are of consent and sufferance in* have agreed and been accessory to

8 *roynish* scurvy

13 *wrestler* (probably three syllables)

17 *that gallant* (Orlando)

19 *suddenly* immediately

20 *quail* (usually explained as 'slacken' but may well retain its usual meaning of 'cower', 'shrink back because afraid')

I.3.3 *memory* memorial

4 *make you* are you doing

7 *so fond to* so foolish as to

8 *bonny prizer* big (or strong) prize-fighter

15 *Envenoms* poisons; but Adam seems to mean that Orlando's bravery has led people like the Duke to treat him as if he were poisonous or dangerous. There is probably a reference to the poisoned garment that Deianira was tricked into giving to Hercules. (The story is told by Ovid in the *Metamorphoses*, Book IX, lines 138 ff.)

23 *use* are accustomed

26 *practices* plots

27 *place* dwelling, home. (Shakespeare's own house in Stratford was called 'New Place'.)

30 *so* provided that

32 *boisterous* violent

enforce gain by force

37 *diverted blood* a relationship turned away from its natural course (perhaps a kind of pun, for physicians also 'diverted' real blood)

39 *thrifty hire I saved* wages I, thriftily, saved

42 *thrown* lie thrown, or be thrown

43, 44 *He that doth the ravens feed, | . . . the sparrow*. Shakespeare may be thinking of any one of a number of Biblical passages (for example, Psalms 147.9, Matthew 10.29, Luke 12.6–7). Compare Hamlet's *there is a special providence in the fall of a sparrow* (V.2.212–13).

47 *lusty* vigorous (*not* 'lustful')

49 *rebellious* (probably) causing rebellion (in the body)

53 *kindly*. This means either 'beneficial' or '(only insofar) as it ought to be in the ordinary course of nature'.

57 *antique* ancient, former. This is perhaps not the same word as *antick* in II.1.31, although the variation in the F spellings – 'anticke', 'antique' – may be due merely to the two different compositors ('C' and 'D') who set up the sections.

58 *sweat* (the past tense)

meed reward. Furness recorded that his copy of F read 'neede', which also makes good sense; but inspection reveals that somebody (probably a previous owner) had altered the word by erasing a minim.

61 *choke their service up*. This somewhat unusual phrase probably has a Biblical origin, in Matthew 13.22: the Bishops' Bible reads 'the care of this world, and the deceitfulness of riches, choke up the word', where a gardening metaphor is being used. The meaning would thus be that the services are choked out of existence by

	the promotion gained. Another gardening metaphor follows in lines 63–5.
65	*lieu of* return for
68	*low* humble
69	*thee*. This is the first time Adam presumes to use the familiar form. See Introduction, page 33.
71	*seventeen*. F's 'seauentie' is an obvious slip, for it has 'seauenteene' in line 73.
74	*a week*. The modern idiom is 'in the day'. Alternatively the phrase may mean, in ironic understatement, 'too late by a week'.
II.4	(stage direction) *alias Touchstone*. See Introduction, page 16.
1	*weary*. F's 'merry' must be an error (perhaps the manuscript read 'wery'). Rosalind can hardly be pretending to be merry, to encourage Celia, for Touchstone seems to catch up the word *weary* in his reply.
6	*weaker vessel*. The phrase is, of course, Biblical (1 Peter 3.7) and indeed Rosalind's following words are a kind of jocular paraphrase of that verse.
	doublet-and-hose jacket and knee-breeches (normal Elizabethan male dress)
10	*no cross*. A pun and not an original one: (1) no trouble; (2) no coin (some coins had a cross on one side). There may, however, be a further pun on Matthew 10.38 ('And he that taketh not his cross, and followeth, is not worthy of me') or the comparable Luke 14.27.
16–17	*Ay, be so . . . | . . . solemn talk*. The lines are printed as prose in F but (if *Ay* is treated as extrametrical, in the normal way) make good verse. They mark the modulation to the verse of the Corin–Silvius exchange, and Rosalind's lines 40–41 modulate from that verse back to Touchstone's prose.
27	*fantasy* fancy, affection (not used pejoratively)
34	*Wearing*. Perhaps this was a variant of 'wearying';

perhaps it was a Shakespearian, or Warwickshire, spelling of 'wearying'; more probably it *means* 'wearing (out)'.

40 *searching of* (in) probing (a medical term)

41 *hard adventure* painful experience

45 *batler* (the wooden club used for beating clothes in the process of washing them)

46 *chopt* chapped

47 *peascod.* The peascod or pea-pod was associated with several rustic superstitions in connexion with wooing and was an appropriate 'lucky' gift. No doubt there are the usual quibbles throughout this passage on 'peas', 'cods' (compare 'codpiece') and possibly 'sword' and 'stone'.

51 *mortal in folly* foolish as only a mortal can be – unless it means 'mortally, extremely, foolish' (but that would seem to be a later use). Perhaps Rosalind takes *mortal* in the sense of 'fatal'.

52, 53 *ware.* Another pun: (1) aware; (2) wary, frightened.

53 *Nay* indeed (not implying contradiction)

55–6 *passion* | ... *fashion.* The rhyme suggests that Rosalind is quoting, perhaps from a ballad, unless she is parodying Silvius's style.

57 *something* somewhat

69 *entertainment* provision for the needs of a guest

78 *recks to find* cares about finding. (F's 'wreakes' probably signifies only a different pronunciation.) In lines 77–9 Shakespeare may be thinking of the story of Nabal in 1 Samuel 25.

80 *cote* cottage

bounds of feed full extent of his pastures

81 *on sale* in the process of being sold (as lines 85–7 make clear)

84 *in my voice* so far as my voice or decision is concerned

85 *What* who

86 *but erewhile* only a short time ago

88 *stand with honesty* is not inconsistent with fair dealing

90 *to pay for it* something with which to pay for it
91 *mend* amend, improve
92 *waste* pass
94 *upon report* after hearing details
96 *feeder* servant

II.5 (stage direction) *others* (in stage practice, usually a group of attendant lords)
1 AMIENS. F has the simple heading 'Song' but the following dialogue leaves no doubt that Amiens is the singer.
3 *turn* adapt
14 *ragged* hoarse
19–20 *I care not for their names, they owe me nothing.* This is normally taken as a quibble on *names*, in the sense of signatures on a legal document acknowledging a debt.
23 *that* that which
24 *dog-apes* dog-faced baboons
26 *beggarly* to be expected from a beggar
28 *cover the while* in the meantime lay the covers (the utensils for a meal), 'set the table'
30 *look you* seek you, look for you (not an error but a regular transitive use of the verb)
32 *disputable* argumentative, disputatious
36 *to live i'th'sun* to live the free, irresponsible life of 'nature'
43 *note* melody
44 *in despite of my invention* to spite my (lack of) inventiveness, to prove that 'invention' isn't necessary for the composition of nonsense
46 JAQUES. F heads this speech also '*Amy.*' (Amiens) – but he can hardly have three consecutive speeches. It would be possible for Jaques to say only *Thus it goes*, handing Amiens a sheet of paper, and for Amiens both to sing Jaques's words and to ask about *ducdame.*
51 *Ducdame.* 'Explanations' range from a Latin phrase to an Italian to a Welsh to a Romani (all of course slightly

adjusted) but Jaques gives the best explanation: the word is deliberate nonsense, which will incite fools to form a circle ('go into a huddle'!).

54 *An if* if

56 *Greek* meaningless ('it's all Greek to me')

58 *first-born of Egypt*. The words are, of course, from Exodus 11.5 and 12.12 and 29, but their relevance is not obvious, even if Jaques is comparing the Duke's banishment with the journey of the Israelites into the wilderness after the first-born of Egypt had been slain by the Lord.

59 *banquet*. This is probably used in the alternative sense of a light meal, particularly of fruit etc. The meal may have been laid out in the inner stage, if any, or at the rear or side of the stage; no Elizabethan audience would have been worried that Orlando and Adam do not see it in the next 'scene'.

II.6.5 *comfort* comfort thyself, take comfort

6 *uncouth* unknown, or wild, desolate

7 *conceit* imagination

9 *comfortable* comforted, of good comfort

10 *presently* immediately

13 *Well said!* Well done!

cheerly cheerful. F's 'cheerely' may conceivably be 'cheerily'.

II.7 (stage direction) *Enter Duke Senior, Amiens . . . outlaws.* F has '*Enter Duke Sen. & Lord, like Out-lawes*'. One assumes that 'Lords' is intended, and that they include Amiens, who went off to find the Duke at the end of II.5 and who, as the singer of the company, presumably sings *Blow, blow, thou winter wind*. But though the Duke says *Give us some music and, good cousin, sing*, the song is simply headed 'Song', with no name, so that all this is mere inference. It is improbable that '*like Out-lawes*' here points to a different costume from the '*like Forresters*' of II.1.

3 *but even now* only a moment ago

5 *compact of jars* made up of discords

6 *discord in the spheres.* This alludes to the Pythagorean belief, beautifully expounded in *The Merchant of Venice* V.1.60 ff.: *There's not the smallest orb which thou beholdest | But in his motion like an angel sings . . .*, the notes of the individual planets, or of their spheres, combining to form the heavenly 'harmony'. Such harmony was one of the basic principles of the universe – and would need to be reversed before Jaques could become 'musical'.

13 *motley.* Leslie Hotson has argued that the motley of the Elizabethan fool, including the professional fool, was not, as modern producers believe, breeches and hose quartered like racing colours, but the long robe or petticoat, made of cloth woven from threads of mixed colours, and most often basically green or brown. Alternatively, each robe may have had a small design woven in colour.

a miserable world. Emendation of this natural parenthesis to 'ah' or 'word' is hardly necessary, even on the theory that *world* is a variant Elizabethan spelling of 'word'.

19 *Call me not fool till heaven hath sent me fortune* (a development of the proverbial 'fortune favours fools')

20 *dial* (either a watch or the common pocket sun-dial)

poke pocket, wallet or bag. Hotson sees a reference to a standard joke that the fool's coat was itself his cloak-bag, in which he could conveniently be carried off.

28 *And thereby hangs a tale* and more could be said. (The phrase was a cliché.) Some critics have read this passage to mean that Touchstone was parodying Jaques, who does not see that the joke is on him, but there is no good reason for thinking so. What is quite likely is that

Jaques is enjoying indecent puns by Touchstone on *hour* (pronounced like 'whore') and 'tail'.

29 *moral*. Perhaps a verb ('moralize'), more probably an adjective ('moralistic').

30 *Chanticleer* (the cock in the traditional story of Reynard the Fox)

32 *sans intermission* without pause. *Intermission* is to be pronounced as five syllables, and *sans* probably as if it were an English word.

39 *dry as the remainder biscuit*. The brain of an idiot was thought to be hard and dry; and nothing could be harder than would have been the seamen's biscuits left over after a long Elizabethan voyage. Compare III.2. 190–91.

40 *places*. Perhaps a kind of pun, with the second meaning of 'extracts', quotations learned off by heart.

41 *observation* (again five syllables, and probably has the older sense of 'maxim' or 'comment')

44 *suit*. Another pun: (1) petition; (2) clothing; and this in turn suggests the pun in the next line on *weed*. This is one of the image sequences that occur several times in Shakespeare's plays. (It was first noticed by Walter Whiter.)

52 *why . . . way* (perhaps another atrocious pun)

53–5 *He that a fool doth very wisely hit | . . . of the bob*. If Theobald's emendation of F is adopted (the addition of *Not to* to line 55, to complete both metre and sense) the lines mean: 'a man on whom a fool, in his fool's wisdom, scores a hit, is very foolish – even if he smarts under the criticism – if he does not pretend to be insensible of it'. Other bare possibilities are to punctuate 'Doth, very foolishly although he smart, | Seem . . .' or to explain 'the *wise* man appears to be foolish *and to be* insensitive'. *Bob* meant 'bitter jest', 'gibe' but may also be used metaphorically: 'rap over the fingers'.

56 *anatomized* dissected

57 *squandering glances* random hits

58–61 *Invest me in my motley ... | ... my medicine.* These are the lines, together with 47–9 and 70–87, that have been thought by some to allude to Ben Jonson (see Introduction, page 15). Jonson's boast in the Induction to *Every Man out of his Humour*, 'With an armèd and resolvèd hand, | I'll strip the raggèd follies of the time | Naked as at their birth', is certainly similar in tone. There are other parallels not only in Jonson's work but also in Marston's. Jaques is, then, speaking in the language of the best satirists of the period, and in lines 70–87 is making the satirist's usual defence of his satire.

63 *for a counter* in exchange for a mere imitation coin (which I will give you for telling me)

66 *sting* sexual lust

67 *embossèd* protuberant

headed having come to a head, like boils (and *evils* may mean 'carbuncles' or 'eruptions of the skin': the 'King's evil' was scrofula)

68 *caught* (almost a pun: 'caught' as one catches a cold and as one catches a bur in clothing. Compare I.3.14–15.)

70–87 For the topical relevance of this speech, see note on lines 58–61 above. The 'incompleteness' of line 70 does not point to textual corruption: there are many other such lines in Shakespeare.

73 *Till that the weary very means do ebb.* This is a notorious crux but no satisfactory emendation has been proposed. A meaning can be extracted: 'Until the very means (wealth, on which pride is based), being exhausted, may be said to run out as the tide does'.

76 *cost of* wealth needed to maintain

79 *function* office, occupation

80 *That says his bravery is not on my cost* who says his fine clothes are not bought at my expense (that is, tells me to mind my own business and not criticize him). The image link of *bravery* and *suits* is again worthy of note.

82 *mettle* substance, spirit

84 *do him right* describes him correctly

85 *free* guiltless

86 *taxing* criticism

95 *touched my vein* diagnosed my motive or state of mind

97 *inland* near the centre of civilization (as opposed to 'country bred')

98 *nurture* manners, culture

101–2 *An you will not be answered with reason, I must die.* The attempt to make these lines scan as verse is misguided: the drop into prose emphasizes the laconic nature of Jaques's reply. It is customary on the stage for him to nibble something as he says these words – an apple, or even a date, grape, or raisin in deference to the editors who have suspected the 'reason' – 'raisin' quibble, as in Falstaff's *If reasons were as plentiful as blackberries* (*1 Henry IV*, II.4.231).

103–4 *Your gentleness shall force, | ... to gentleness.* The phrase is probably proverbial; a similar one has been found in Publilius Syrus's *Sententiae.*

112 *melancholy* (because they shut out the sunshine)

113 *Lose and neglect* pass, without worrying about them

115 *knolled* rung, pealed (but with no implication of mournfulness)

126 *upon command* at your will or pleasure

127 *wanting* needs

133 *weak* weakening, causing weakness

136 *your good comfort* the goodness and kindness you have shown

140–67 *All the world's a stage, | ... sans everything.* On the background to this famous speech, see Introduction, pages 14–15. There is even a passage in the old play of *Damon and Pithias*, 'Pythagoras said, that this world was like a stage, | Whereon many play their parts'. Shakespeare's originality is in the development of the idea and in the tone, appropriate to Jaques.

145 *Mewling.* Not just 'whimpering' (a meaning that may derive from misunderstanding of this passage) but 'mewing like a cat'.

147 *creeping like snail.* This image may not have come from Shakespeare's memories of Warwickshire after all, even if he was thinking of his schooldays, for Nashe has in *The First Part of Pasquil's Apology* (1590), speaking of contemporary scholars, 'I wonder how these silly snails, creeping but yesterday out of shops and Grammar-schools, dare thrust out their feeble horns, against so tough and mighty adversaries' (as their predecessors).

149 *woeful* full of woe

151 *pard* panther or leopard

152 *Jealous in honour* quick to take offence in matters thought to concern his honour

155 *capon* chicken (and 'capon-justice' was the regular term for one who could be bribed with such a gift)

157 *saws* sayings

modern instances trite or commonplace (*not* 'up-to-date') illustrations

159 *pantaloon* (the dotard of Italian comedy)

161 *hose* breeches

165 *history* history-play, chronicle

166 *mere* complete

167 (stage direction) *Enter Orlando with Adam.* Capell first recorded the tradition that a contemporary remembered Shakespeare's having played a part, presumably Adam, in which he was carried on the stage on another's back.

180 *rude* rough

181 *Hey-ho.* This is common in refrains and though spelt 'Heigh ho' in F does not necessarily refer to a sigh.

holly (associated with rejoicing and festivities)

182 *Most friendship . . . mere folly.* Perhaps this too is a proverb.

197 *effigies.* This is an alternative, singular, form of 'effigy' (meaning 'image') and is stressed on the second syllable.

198 *limned* portrayed, or reproduced

III.1.2 *the better part made mercy* for the greater part so merciful by disposition

3 *argument* subject

6 *Seek him with candle.* The reference (coming ironically from the Duke) is to Luke 15.8, 'What woman, having ten pieces of silver, if she lose one, doth not light a candle, and sweep the house, and seek diligently till she find it?' (the verse that follows 'joy shall be in heaven over one sinner that repenteth . . .').

7 *turn* return

10 *seize.* Perhaps in the sense of 'seise' (take legal possession of); *extent* in line 17 is the legal term for a writ for taking the initial steps in the seising of land as security for debt etc.

11 *quit* acquit

mouth (that is, words, evidence)

16 *of such a nature* whose duty it is to do this

18 *expediently* in haste, expeditiously

turn him going 'set him packing'

III.2.1 *Hang there.* No doubt one of the pillars supporting the 'heavens' over the bare Elizabethan public stage would serve well enough for a tree (Rosalind says later that she found Orlando's poem *on a tree*). Hanging love poems (or carving names) on trees was part of the traditional behaviour of the pastoral lover.

2 *thrice-crownèd.* Diana (Artemis), the goddess of chastity, was identified with Proserpina (Hecate) in the underworld and with Luna (Selene) in the sky; alternatively, the passage suggests three functions of Diana: goddess of the moon (line 2), of chastity (line 3), and of the hunt (line 4).

4 *Thy huntress' name.* Rosalind is thought of as a nymph in Diana's train because she too is chaste.

sway control

6 *character* inscribe

10 *unexpressive* inexpressible

15 *naught* worthless

16 *private* secluded; not public. (The contrast between *solitary* and *private* is none too clear.)

18 *spare* frugal

19 *humour* temperament, or mood. (Compare 'I am not in the humour'.)

23 *wants* lacks

28 *complain of good breeding* complain that he has been denied good upbringing or birth

30 *natural philosopher* (1) a philosopher who studies nature; (2) a foolish pretender to thought

35–6 *damned . . . on one side.* A comparable modern idiom is 'half-baked'.

39 *manners.* Another quibble: (1) forms of polite behaviour; (2) morals.

46 *salute* greet

but unless

49 *Instance* (give an) example

50 *still* constantly

fells fleeces

61 *civet* the perfume obtained (as Touchstone is quick to point out) from the *flux* or glandular secretion of the civet cat

62 *worms' meat* food for worms, a mere corpse. (Mercutio in *Romeo and Juliet*, III.1.107, when stabbed, says *They have made worms' meat of me.*)

62–3 *in respect of* in comparison with

64 *perpend* consider, weigh the facts

68 *God make incision . . . raw!* Two explanations have been offered, one from surgery (blood-letting to cure soreness or sickness), one from gardening (grafting to improve what is *raw* or wild).

69 *get* earn

71 *content with my harm* patient under my misfortunes

76–7 *bell-wether* the leading sheep of the flock (obviously here a ram, *not* a castrated male) on whose neck a bell was hung

84 *Ind* Indies. It was, often at least, pronounced to rhyme with 'lined'. But the suggestion may be that Orlando is straining for rhymes.

88 *lined* drawn (but the word is also used, as Touchstone uses it in line 101, of the male dog covering the bitch)

94 *right butter-women's rank to market* the genuine movement of the butter-women jogging along to the market. Perhaps there is also a picture of the butter-women in a rank or line, at regular intervals, but the later phrase *false gallop* makes it probable that *rank* here means 'pace' or 'jog-trot'. Both phrases may be reminiscences of a passage in Nashe's *Strange News* (1592): 'I would trot a false gallop through the rest of his ragged verses, but that if I should report his rhyme doggerel aright I must make my verses, as he doth his, run hobbling like a brewer's cart upon the stones, and observe no length in their feet.'

99 *kind* its own kin or species

101 *Wintered* used in winter

103–4 *They that reap ... cart with Rosalind.* Touchstone's parody is far from genteel: 'Those that sow must reap, and so Rosalind must pay the cost of what she has done – by being carted like a prostitute'. Public exposure in, and whipping at the rear of, a cart was the regular punishment.

113 *graff* graft (which is a later form of the word). Perhaps there is a pun on *you* and 'yew', and reference to Matthew 7.17–18: '... a corrupt tree bringeth forth evil fruit ...'.

114 *medlar* the tree bearing the apple-like fruit which is fit for eating only when decayed. There is also a pun, of course, on 'meddler': Touchstone is interfering.

114–15 *then it will be the earliest fruit i'th'country* the fruit of the medlar (which normally bears late in the season) will then be rotten far sooner (and rottenness is the *right virtue* or true merit of the medlar)

121–2 *Why should this ... unpeopled? No.* Some editors have defended F's 'Desert' against Rowe's emendation 'a desert', but Orlando's versification is mostly jingle. F has a comma after *be*, but probably a question is intended: 'Why should this be a desert? Because it is unpeopled? No.' It could be argued, however, that the comma makes slightly better sense of Orlando's lame poem as a whole: 'Why should lack of people make this a desert? I'll put tongues on every tree and solve that difficulty.'

124 *civil sayings* maxims appropriate to civilization (as against deserts)

126 *erring* wandering (with no sense of error)

127–8 *the stretching of a span ... sum of age.* A span is the distance measured by thumb and little finger, and Shakespeare is no doubt alluding to Psalm 39.5, 'Thou hast made my days as it were an hand breadth long' ('span' in the Prayer Book).

128 *Buckles in* encloses

135 *quintessence.* The quintessence was the fifth 'essence' (additional to the four elements) of which heavenly bodies were thought to be composed and which was latent in everything; astrologers aimed at isolating it by distillation (line 140), in a search for the secrets of transmutation.

sprite spirit

136 *in little* in the little world of man, the microcosm, of which every part corresponded to something in the universe, or macrocosm

137 *Heaven Nature charged* Heaven gave orders to Nature

139 *wide-enlarged* endowed in fullest measure

140 *presently* immediately

141 *Helen's cheek* the beautiful complexion or face of Helen of Troy

143 *better part.* Probably Atalanta's 'grace' or her 'physique' (since she was such a splendid runner – compare lines 268–9), but the meaning is in dispute. Another suggestion is Atalanta's 'determination to remain chaste'.

144 *Sad Lucretia's modesty*. Lucretia killed herself after she was violated by Tarquin. *Sad* means 'serious'.

146 *synod* (probably used here in its astrological sense of 'conjunction')

148 *touches* traits

151 *Jupiter*. The generally accepted emendation to 'pulpiter' (preacher) is gratuitous. Rosalind swears by Jupiter and by Jove in II.2 and is no doubt comparing and contrasting the poet, or Celia who reads his poem, with the not-so-gentle voice of Jupiter speaking from Heaven.

154 *How now? Back, friends*. It seems more likely that Celia is telling Corin and Touchstone to stand back than that she puns on 'back-friends' – (1) false friends; (2) people standing behind her back, whom she now sees for the first time.

157–8 *bag and baggage . . . scrip and scrippage*. To be allowed to depart with one's bags and their contents was an honourable condition on which to surrender; Touchstone and Corin may have no bags, but Corin has the shepherd's pouch (the *scrip*) and Touchstone, presumably, the fool's wallet. *Baggage* already meant also a strumpet (and Touchstone has just made his uncomplimentary comparison of Rosalind with a prostitute) and so *scrippage* (a word he invents for the contents of the scrip) may be better worth having than baggage.

168 *should be* came to be

169 *seven of the nine days*. The phrase depends on the proverbial 'a nine days' wonder'.

171–2 *I was never . . . hardly remember*. Rosalind jokingly pretends to accept two wild beliefs: Pythagoras's doctrine of the transmigration of souls, and the Irish superstition that rats could be killed with rhymes used as spells.

172 *that* in that; when

173 *Trow you* do you know

178–80 *it is a hard matter . . . so encounter*. There is an old proverb 'Friends may meet but mountains never greet'.

182 *Is it possible?* (that is, possible that you don't know)
186–7 *out of all whooping* far beyond what all cries of astonishment can express
188 *Good my complexion!* pardon my blushes
189 *caparisoned* dressed, decked out
190–91 *a South Sea of discovery* as tedious as a voyage of discovery in the interminable South Seas
192 *apace* rapidly, or immediately
203 *stay* wait for
207–8 *sad brow and true maid* with a serious face and on your honour as a virgin
214 *Wherein went he?* in what clothes was he dressed?
215 *makes he* is he doing
218 *Gargantua* the giant of fairy-tale (and of Rabelais's famous story)
225 *atomies* motes, specks
225–6 *resolve the propositions of* solve the problems put forward for solution by
227 *relish it with good observance* sauce it and make it more palatable, by paying respectful attention
229 *Jove's tree* the oak (sacred to Jove)
231 *Give me audience* let me do the talking
233–4 *There lay he ... wounded knight.* Celia is possibly adopting the language of the fashionable romance.
235–6 *well becomes the ground* befits the earth (with a quibble on *ground* meaning 'background')
237 *holla* whoa! The image is carried on in *curvets*: 'leaps about like a frisky horse'.
238 *furnished* dressed (as also in V.4.204)
239 *heart* (with a pun on 'hart')
240 *burden.* The word was used both of the refrain and of the bass or undersong. Compare IV.2.13 and note.
244 *bring me out* put me out
250 *God buy you* God be with you (our 'good-bye')
254 *moe* more. It is not clear why Orlando is given this older form when Jaques uses *more*.
255 *ill-favouredly* badly; or with a disapproving expression

257 *just* exactly, quite so

264–5 *conned them out of rings* learned them by heart from rings (in which posies were inscribed)

266 *right painted cloth* in the authentic manner of painted cloth (the cheaper alternative to tapestry), on which were painted scriptural and other texts

272 *breather* ('man alive' in modern idiom)

281 *There I shall see mine own figure.* As Furness said, the line is unworthy of Jaques!

304 *trots hard* moves at an uncomfortable jog-trot

313 *wasteful* (perhaps) causing to waste away

316–17 *go as softly* walk as slowly

319 *stays* stands

327 *cony* rabbit

328 *kindled* born

330 *purchase* acquire

removed remote

332 *religious uncle* uncle who was a member of a religious order. Some editors, implausibly, have suggested some connexion between this supposed *religious uncle* and the *old religious man* of V.4.157.

333 *inland* city, cultured. Compare II.7.97 and note.

courtship (1) court life; (2) wooing

336 *touched with* stained with; or accused of

344–5 *I will not cast away ... are sick.* There may be an allusion to Matthew 9.12: 'They that be whole need not the physician, but they that are sick'.

349 *fancy-monger* one who deals in love (as a woodmonger deals in wood)

350 *quotidian* daily, recurrent fever

356 *rushes* reeds. Rosalind is implying that it is easy to escape from the cage of love.

358 *blue eye* eye with dark rings around it. On this paragraph, see Introduction, pages 27–8.

359 *unquestionable* not to be spoken to

361–2 *simply your having* the little you have

364 *unbanded* without a coloured hat-band

365–6 *careless desolation* despondency beyond caring

367 *point-device* fastidiously precise (shortened from 'at point device', from French *à point devis*)

374 *still* always

376 *admired* marvelled at

383 *merely* completely (similarly in line 402, and compare *mere oblivion* in II.7.166)

384 *dark house and a whip.* Rosalind is not inventing the punishment. This was a common Elizabethan treatment for the insane, as the trick played on Malvolio in *Twelfth Night* shows.

386 *ordinary* common, frequent

392 *moonish* changeable (like the moon)

397 *entertain* receive kindly

399 *that* with the result that

drave drove (a common form of the past tense)

400 *living* real, authentic, not put on for the occasion. (Othello asks for *a living reason* of Desdemona's guilt.)

403 *liver.* This was thought to be the seat of the passions.

411–12 *by the way* on the way

III.3.3 *feature* form (or, judging by Touchstone's next lines, 'conduct'); but presumably Audrey suspects an innuendo

4 *warrant* protect

6–7 *capricious . . . Goths.* There is a series of learned puns here. *Capricious* is derived from the Latin word *caper* (goat) and originally meant 'goat-like' and 'lascivious'; *Goths* was pronounced like 'goats'; and Ovid, who was exiled from Rome and forced to live among the Goths, was renowned not for being *honest* (pure) but as the author of some very licentious poems: indeed, his banishment was possibly due either to his *Ars Amatoria* or to his liaison with the Emperor's daughter Julia. All this is wasted on Audrey, of course, but not on Jaques.

8 *ill-inhabited* badly housed

8–9 *Jove in a thatched house*. Jaques also has his classical learning. He refers to the time when Jove, in disguise, visited the earth and was warmly entertained by the poor old couple Baucis and Philemon, in their humble cottage.

11 *seconded with* supported by

12–13 *it strikes . . . in a little room*. For the possible reference to the death of Marlowe, see Introduction, pages 36–7. A *little room* may mean a private one in an inn, in which the *reckoning* ('bill for a meal') would be more likely to be unreasonable.

19 *may be said*. Mason's emendation 'it may be said' perhaps makes the sense a little clearer, but Touchstone is merely playing with words. There may be a pun on *feign* meaning 'pretend' and 'fain' meaning 'desire'.

26 *hard-favoured* ugly

29 *material* full of matter; or practical, unromantic

35 *foul*. Perhaps to Audrey the word means only 'plain' ('homely' in the current American usage).

38–9 *Sir Oliver Martext*. *Martext* is a type-name, of the kind frequently used in anti-Puritan pamphlets; and *Sir* seems to have been the normal 'title' for an unlettered country clergyman.

46 *horn-beasts*. There is the usual quibble on 'animals with horns' and 'cuckolds'. F's 'horne' may be a misreading of 'hornd', but the sense is not affected.

46–7 *what though?* what of it?

51 *Poor men alone?* Whether one retains the F punctuation ('euen so poore men alone:') or interprets as in the given text, the sense is clear: Touchstone himself raises, and rejects, the supposition that only poor men's wives are unfaithful.

52 *rascal* poorer deer of the herd

58 *want* be without (but there is another learned quibble because of the 'horn of plenty')

68 *'ild* reward (abbreviation of 'yield' in its original meaning). So too in V.4.53.

69 *your last company* your latest company ('your action in joining us now')

70 *toy* matter of no great importance

be covered replace your hat. Here, and to William in V.1.16–17, Touchstone condescendingly speaks as the monarch or nobleman normally speaks to the inferior who has thus shown a mark of respect – but the respect was being paid by Jaques to the clergyman's office, not to Touchstone.

72 *bow* yoke (or part inserted in it)

79 *wainscot* wooden panelling

panel. If, as has been suggested, *panel* could also mean 'prostitute', *warp* may also have the secondary meaning of 'go wrong'.

81 *not in the mind but.* This must be the double negative that does make an affirmative: 'inclined to think that'.

85 *me ... thee.* Jaques's internal rhyme may be unintentional, but Touchstone caps it with a deliberate one *Audrey ... bawdry.* F sets the lines out as verse.

89–95 *O sweet Oliver.* Touchstone sings part of, and parodies, a popular ballad, which is believed to have been sung to the tune of 'In peascod time'. See 'The Songs', page 199.

.4.6 *dissembling colour* (red; or, as line 10 has it, *chestnut*: the traditional colour of Judas's hair and therefore the sign of hypocrisy)

10 *your chestnut* (*not* Rosalind's, but 'the chestnut we are talking about')

13 *holy bread.* This was originally the bread that was blessed and distributed to those who had *not* taken Communion, but after the Reformation it came to mean sacramental bread. (Interestingly the phrase was expunged by a seventeenth-century Catholic priest censoring a copy of the Second Folio to be used by English students at Valladolid in Spain.)

14 *cast lips of Diana* lips cast for a statue of Diana, the goddess of chastity. (The alternative interpretation, 'cast off', seems almost ludicrous.)

15 *of winter's sisterhood.* That is to say, extremely 'cold' or chaste

23 *concave* hollow

28 *tapster* waiter, or drawer of ale, in an inn, who would also make up the *reckonings* ('bills')

32 *question* conversation

34 *what* why

36 *brave* fine

36–40 *He ... swears brave oaths ... noble goose.* Orlando's oaths merely glance off the heart of his loved one, just as an insignificant (or, perhaps, 'unskilled') knight, who in tilting spurs his horse only on one side, breaks his lance like a coward, with a glancing blow (instead of hitting his target in the centre)

43 *complained of* uttered his lament about

51 *remove* go, move off

III.5.5 *Falls* drops

6 *But first begs* without first begging

11 *sure* surely

13 *atomies* motes (as before in III.2.225)

23 *cicatrice and capable impressure* scar-like mark and perceptible imprint

29 *fancy* love

38–9 *no more in you | ... to bed.* Rosalind means that Phebe's beauty alone would not light up the room and make a candle unnecessary.

42 *ordinary* ordinary run

43 *sale-work* ready-made goods (inferior to more careful work)

'Od's (an abbreviation of 'may God save')

47 *bugle* bead-like. A bugle was a glass bead, usually black (and Phebe's eyes are black according to line 130).

50 *south* south wind

51 *properer* more handsome (as again in line 55)

53 *ill-favoured* ugly

61 *Cry the man mercy* beg the man's forgiveness

62 *Foul is most foul . . . a scoffer* ugliness is most ugly when the ugliness is in being a scoffer (with 'wicked' as a secondary meaning of *foul*)

66–7 *He's fallen . . . my anger.* Some editors think these lines are an aside, but Rosalind is not concerned to spare Phebe's feelings.

69 *sauce* rebuke, sting

78 *see* see you

79 *abused* deceived

81 *saw* maxim. For this quotation from Marlowe's *Hero and Leander*, see Introduction, page 37.

89 *extermined* destroyed, ended

90 *neighbourly* (in accordance with the injunction to love one's neighbour as oneself)

93 *it is not that* the time has not yet come

95 *erst* not long ago

irksome hateful, offensive

100 *in such a poverty of grace.* That is, because so little grace has been shown, or given, to him.

104 *scattered* random

107 *bounds* lands (on which he had the right of pasturage)

108 *carlot* peasant, churl. (The word is not recorded elsewhere, but 'carl' is, in the same sense.)

123 *damask.* The reference may be to the damask rose or to the woven fabric.

125 *In parcels* feature by feature

132 *answered not again* did not answer back

133 *omittance is no quittance.* This is a proverb: 'failure to do something at the time is not a full discharge from the responsibility of doing it in the long run'.

136 *straight* immediately

138 *passing short* extremely curt

IV.1.3 *melancholy fellow.* There is, no doubt, topical humour here: a pose of melancholy seems to have been fashionable in the 1590s and early seventeenth century, and many dramatists refer to it. The man who adopted the pose could always claim that black bile predominated in his make-up and made his 'humour' inevitable. (Compare *humorous* in line 18.) Fashionable modern 'complexes' provide the perfect parallel.

6 *abominable*. The F spelling 'abhominable' probably preserves the false etymology *ab homine* and so the second sense of 'not human'.

7 *modern* everyday (as in II.7.157)

8 *sad* solemn

13 *politic* crafty, guided by considerations only of expediency

14 *nice* (pretending to be) fastidious

16 *simples* ingredients

26 *travail* (1) work hard; (2) travel

28 (stage direction) *Going*. F does not mark an 'exit' for Jaques, but obviously Rosalind should not deign to notice Orlando, who has come late for his appointment, until Jaques, who has begun to leave as he speaks his farewell, is off stage; she continues talking to Jaques as he goes.

30 *lisp* affect a foreign accent (Rosalind's list of complaints against returned travellers echoes many others in Elizabethan writing)

disable belittle

33 *swam* floated (an alternative form of the past participle). The gibe has the further point that Venice was the goal of many Elizabethan travellers, partly because it was notorious for its prostitutes.

42–3 *clapped him o'th'shoulder* arrested him or claimed him as his own

49 *jointure* marriage-settlement

55 *prevents* anticipates

slander disgrace (rather than 'evil report' in the modern sense)

60 *leer* complexion (the restricted meaning 'sly look' seems to have developed later)

67 *gravelled* perplexed, at a loss (a similar modern image is 'stranded')

68 *out* at a loss

69 *warn* summon (although Onions and others believe it to be a variant of 'warrant')

77 *honesty* virtue, chastity

ranker more suspect (but some editors paraphrase as 'stronger')

78 *of* out of (and Rosalind proceeds to pun on *suit* in the senses of 'suit of clothes' and 'courting' and possibly even 'law suit')

85 *by attorney* by proxy (as in 'power of attorney')

87 *videlicet* namely (Rosalind is continuing the legal language begun by *attorney* or *suit*)

89 *Grecian club*. There are various versions of how Troilus, the prototype of the true lover, met his death; this is Rosalind's own. (Shakespeare's *Troilus and Cressida* does not carry the story to the death of Troilus but has him fling himself recklessly into battle when he discovers Cressida to be false.)

90 *Leander*. According to the accepted version of the story, he swam the Hellespont every night to visit Hero in Sestos (and was drowned).

119 *Go to* (not an abbreviation, but an exclamation of mild or simulated impatience)

127 *commission* authority. This exchange of vows may have had even greater significance for an Elizabethan audience, since such a declaration, before a third party, constituted one kind of legal marriage contract.

129 *goes before* anticipates (because, for one thing, she has not waited to be asked 'Will you ...?')

139 *Barbary* a breed introduced from Barbary, the 'Barb' (apparently its origin is enough to imply jealousy)

140 *against* anticipating, predicting

new-fangled readily distracted by every novelty

142 *Diana in the fountain.* A figure of Diana was the centre of more than one fountain. Shakespeare may or may not have been thinking of the one erected in London in 1596 (it does not seem to have had a *weeping* Diana).

150 *Make* close (a use still found in dialect)

155 *Wit, whither wilt?* For the same joke, see I.2.53-4 and note.

162 *her husband's occasion* the opportunity of finding fault in her husband

171 *but one cast away* only one woman cast off. (Editors have suspected a proverb or quotation from a popular ballad.)

177 *pathetical* affecting; producing strong emotion (not only pity)

180 *gross* whole; or large

185 *try* judge the case

186 *simply misused* completely disgraced

187-9 *We must . . . her own nest.* For the adaptation from Lodge, see Introduction, page 21.

196 *bastard of Venus* Cupid (son of Venus but by Mercury, not by her husband Vulcan)

197 *thought.* It is difficult to say which of many possible shades of meaning the word has here: probably 'fancy' rather than 'melancholy'.

spleen caprice, waywardness

198 *abuses* deceives

IV.2 This charming interlude, which contributes to the pastoral atmosphere (and mocks it), has the added function of marking the passing of the two hours specified in the previous scene.

(stage direction) *Lords dressed as foresters.* The F stage direction is '*Enter Iaques and Lords, Forresters*'. Lines 2 and 7 are given to '*Lord*' and the song is headed simply 'Musicke, Song' with no singer named. Perhaps this time foresters were intended to appear and even to sing, but there would seem to be no need for variation from II.1 and II.7: the Lords would have done the hunting and Jaques could address one of them as *forester* because of the costume. It is not necessary to give Amiens either line 7 or the song, for Jaques's lines 8-9 may envisage singing by the whole group.

12-13 *the rest shall bear | This burden. Burden* does also mean 'chorus' (compare III.2.240 and note) and some editors take these words to be a direction to *the rest* to sing the refrain. But F prints the words in italic, as part of the song; *bear* rhymes with *wear* although F prints '*Then sing . . . burthen*' as one line; and the point of the song is that *all* must run the risk of cuckoldry.

18 *lusty.* This time there is reference to 'lust' in the modern sense: the horn is *lusty* because it is the symbol of the wife's lust as well as the husband's shame.

IV.3.2 *much* (used ironically: compare the modern colloquialism 'a fat lot of . . .')

18 *phoenix.* The point is that only one phoenix, according to the myth, could be alive at any one time; the new bird rose from the ashes of its predecessor.

'Od's my will as God's is my will (or 'God save my will')

24 *turned* brought

26 *freestone* (a fine-grained limestone or sandstone, between brown and yellow in colour)

35 *giant rude.* This is probably a compound adjective: 'incredibly barbarous, on the scale of a giant'.

40 *Phebes me* addresses me in her own style

45 *laid apart* doffed for the time being

49 *vengeance* damage

50 *Meaning me a beast* thereby making me into a beast (since my eye has a different effect from a man's)

51 *eyne* eyes (an old form, used by Shakespeare here as a 'poeticism')

54 *aspect*. Possibly 'look' but more probably this is the astrological term, meaning, roughly, 'phase'.

59 *by him seal up thy mind* use him as messenger to carry a sealed letter in which you state your decision. The alternative explanation, 'make your final decision', hardly explains *by him*.

60 *kind* disposition

62 *make* bring with me; or do

79 *bottom* valley

80 *rank of osiers* row of willows

81 *Left* passed

87 *favour* complexion; or countenance

bestows himself carries himself, has the manner

88 *ripe sister* mature older sister (of the girl Celia). Some editors emend *sister* to 'forester', not very plausibly.

low short (or 'shorter' if *low and browner* is to be construed, in a normal Elizabethan way, as 'lower and browner'). See too Introduction, pages 40–41.

94 *napkin* handkerchief

102 *fancy* love

113 *indented* zigzagging, undulating

117 *When that* for the time when

123 *render* declare, describe (as)

129 *kindness* (probably in both senses: (1) kinship; (2) generosity)

130 *just occasion* legitimate excuse, or perfect opportunity

132 *hurtling* tumult, violent conflict

135 *contrive* scheme

139 *By and by* immediately (the sense is much weaker now)

141 *recountments* narratives of our adventures (the word is the grammatical object of *bathed*)

144 *entertainment* hospitality

151 *Brief* in brief (as in line 143)

recovered revived

166 *a body* anybody, one

170 *passion of earnest* genuine emotion or suffering

V.1.10 *clown* yokel, country bumpkin

12 *shall be flouting* must jeer

hold refrain

13 *even.* F's spelling 'eu'n' may represent a rustic speech, which Touchstone imitates.

14 *God ye* God give you

34 *lips to open.* Perhaps William's mouth is similarly wide open, but with astonishment.

40 *figure* accepted device (such as hyperbole). Touchstone's illustration, of course, is deliberate nonsense.

42 *consent* agree

ipse (Latin for 'he himself')

51 *to wit* that is to say (a legal phrase)

53 *bastinado* beating with a cudgel (as against fencing with steel)

54 *bandy with thee in faction* compete against you in insults and other forms of dissension

55 *policy* 'Machiavellian' policy (using any means to achieve the desired end)

V.2.4 *persever* (an obsolete form of 'persevere', stressed on the second syllable)

5 *giddiness* rashness

11 *estate* settle

14 *all's* all his

18 *sister.* For comment on Oliver's acceptance of the pretence that 'Ganymede' is Rosalind, see Introduction, pages 29–30.

26 *sound* swoon

28 *where you are* what you are referring to

28–39 *there was never anything so sudden . . . part them.* For comment on this passage as an element in the plot, see Introduction, pages 22–3.

30 *thrasonical* in the bragging style of the soldier Thraso, in Terence's *Eunuch* (Shakespeare was certainly not the first to use the word)

36 *degrees.* There is a quibble on *degrees* meaning also

flight (*pair*) of stairs, and another on *incontinent*: (1) in haste; (2) unchaste.

39 *clubs*. Some editors see a reference to the Elizabethan custom of calling 'clubs' when summoning help to break up a street brawl.

50 *Know of me then....* Although some wrong conclusions have been drawn, it has rightly been noted that Rosalind's style changes here to a manner much more formal – some would no doubt say 'ritualistic' – as she begins to adopt the role of manipulator of events. The syntax becomes more involved, the sentences longer – and the audience knows that the time for joking is now over.

51–2 *conceit* understanding

53 *insomuch* in as much as

56 *grace me* add to my own merits or reputation

58 *conversed* associated (or even 'studied')

59 *not damnable* not eligible for damnation (his is not 'black' magic, involving the devil). A magician of the wrong kind might be condemned to death too (hence lines 67–8).

60 *gesture* demeanour

63 *inconvenient* inappropriate, out of place

64–5 *human as she is* in the flesh ('the real Rosalind, not the mere phantom or spirit that you might expect a magician to conjure up')

67 *tender* value

69 *bid* invite

74 *study* aim

75 *despiteful* contemptuous

89 *fantasy* imagination not controlled by reason

91 *observance* humble attention. The repetition of the word in line 93 may be an error, compositor's or author's (in which case one has the hopeless task of guessing what Shakespeare may have written or intended to write); but it is just possible that *all observance* is the best Silvius can do to sum up what he has been saying.

101–2 *Why do you... you?* For the possible plot implications of these lines, and of the modulating into prose, see Introduction, pages 29-30.

104-5 *howling of Irish wolves.* The phrase is perhaps an adaptation of one in Lodge, where Rosalynde tells Montanus that in courting Phoebe he barks 'with the wolves of Syria against the moon' (that is, in vain). Perhaps Shakespeare's wolves are Irish because of the tradition that once a year the Irish were turned into wolves.

V.3 On the dramatic functions of this scene, see Introduction, page 35.

4 *dishonest* unchaste – with a pun, not intended by Audrey, on *woman of the world*, which she uses in its other meaning of 'married woman'. Perhaps there are subtle allusions to Genesis 19.31 and Luke 20.34. *Dishonest* is the opposite of *honest* as used two lines later to mean 'honourable'.

10 *clap into't roundly* strike into it without unnecessary preliminaries

10-11 *hawking* making the customary noises to clear the throat

11-12 *the only prologues* merely the prologues

13 *in a tune.* This may mean either 'keeping time with one another' or 'in unison'.

15-38 *It was a lover. . . .* The best known setting for this song is that by Shakespeare's famous contemporary Thomas Morley (published in his *First Book of Airs*, 1600, of which there is a unique copy in the Folger Shakespeare Library). It is printed on page 200, below. If Morley wrote the music especially for Shakespeare's words (as seems likely from his statement in the Dedication that the airs 'were made this vacation time'), this would be the only known occasion when a Shakespeare song was so set by one of the great school of Elizabethan lutenists; but it is possible that Morley's music (and even the words) preceded the play. The Morley version justifies the re-ordering of the stanzas as in the text (F prints the present last stanza as the second) and the emending of F's '*rang time*' to *ring time*; perhaps it would also justify the omitting of *the* in line 18 (*In the spring time*) to make that part of the first stanza identical with the others (Morley has notes of music only for *In* and *spring*). In line 23 it reads not *country folks* but 'Countrie fooles' and in line 17 has the tempting reading 'corne fields'; on the other hand, it confirms *a life* (as against the emendation 'life') in line 29.

18 *ring time* time for giving or exchanging rings

21 *Between the acres of the rye* (presumably) on the unploughed strips dividing the fields of rye

35 *the prime* perfection (but 'the prime' also meant 'the spring')

40 *the ditty* the words (as opposed to the *note* or music)

41 *untuneable*. Touchstone probably means 'unmusical, even though the words weren't hard to set' or 'ill fitted to the words, insignificant as they were'; but the Pages reply as if he meant either that they both failed to keep proper time or that they did not sing in tune with each other.

V.4.4 *fear they hope, and know they fear* fear that they are only hoping against hope, and know in their hearts that they are afraid

5 *urged* stated formally, and clarified

18 *make all this matter even* smoothe everything out (perhaps with an implied contrast between even and odd). The phrase is curiously echoed in line 25 and again by Hymen in line 106.

21 *Keep you . . . marry me*. It is not true that one has to pronounce *Phebe* as one syllable in order to scan this line, which may be basically trochaic, with a stress on *your*.

26–34 *I do remember . . . this forest.* For comment on the significance of these lines to the plot, see Introduction, page 30.

27 *lively* lifelike; or vivid

touches traits; or strokes (a metaphor from painting)

favour appearance, features, look

32 *desperate* dangerous

34 *Obscurèd* concealed, and protected (as the magician is protected from interference by devils while he is within his magic circle)

35 *toward* on the way

36 *a pair.* The reference is to Genesis 7.2: the Lord told Noah to take with him into the ark seven of each species of 'clean' beast – 'but of unclean cattle two, the male and his female'.

40 *motley-minded* with mind as mixed as the thread of his coat

42–3 *put me to my purgation* give me the chance of clearing myself (compare I.3.51 and note)

43 *measure* a formal aristocratic dance

44 *politic* Machiavellian (compare *policy* in V.1.55)

45 *undone* (by not paying them)

46 *like to have fought* almost fought (the joke being, of course, that courtiers seldom stand to their words when a quarrel becomes serious)

47 *ta'en up* made up (with the consequent avoiding of the duel). The phrase is used again in lines 95–6.

53 *'ild* reward (as in III.3.68)

desire you of the like. This has been variously interpreted: 'I ask permission to return the compliment' or 'I sincerely hope you do think so (and will continue to think so)'.

54–5 *copulatives* those about to be joined, in marriage and carnally

56 *blood breaks* passion wanes

58 *honesty* chastity

61 *swift and sententious* quick-witted and full of wisdom

62 *fool's bolt.* There is a proverb 'a fool's bolt is soon shot'; and perhaps Touchstone is even alluding to the form of bolt or short arrow that was known as a 'quarrel'.

63 *dulcet diseases.* Commentators have tripped over the phrase, but it probably means 'mild or pleasant weaknesses' and refers to the fool's inability to forbear from gibes.

67 *seeming* becomingly

68 *dislike* express disapproval of

69–70 *in the mind* of the opinion that

73 *disabled* belittled (as in IV.1.30)

78–9 *Circumstantial* indirect, the product of circumstance only

84 *measured.* That is, to see that one was not longer than the other (a necessary precaution before the duel).

87 *in print.* There is a quibble here. The phrase also meant 'in a precise way', as did 'by the book': according to the textbook, 'according to Hoyle'. There were textbooks setting out the justifications for duelling, and Shakespeare possibly has a particular one in mind.

95–6 *take up* settle

98–9 *swore brothers* pledged themselves to act like brothers, ever after

103 *stalking-horse* (the horse or, more frequently, imitation horse behind which the hunter sheltered without disturbing the quarry)

104 *presentation.* The *Oxford English Dictionary* takes this as an example of *presentation* meaning a theatrical or symbolic representation or show. It could also mean 'inferior representation', 'mere shadow of the real thing' – and the Duke is saying that Touchstone's folly is only pretended.

(stage direction) *Hymen* (the god of marriage, who was frequently represented in masques). F has simply '*Enter Hymen . . .*' and the producer must make up his mind who plays the part. Some editors think it should be given to the singer who earlier plays Amiens (F does not specify that Hymen's first words are to be sung but does print them in italic). If, as others have maintained, although unnecessarily, the masque was written into the play for a special performance at a wedding, one of the distinguished guests may have been brought in as Hymen. But too much fuss altogether has been made over the masque: it is an appropriate way of arranging weddings, and the stilted verse is not un-Shakespearian but is in the manner of his other masques and interludes, in, for example, *Cymbeline* and *Timon of Athens*.

Still music quiet, peaceful music (such as that of recorders and flutes, not drums and trumpets)

106 *made even*. See line 18 and note.

107 *Atone together* are joined as one, come into accord

111–12 *her hand . . . her bosom*. The F reading, '*his*' in both places, can be justified, if at all, on the ground that Rosalind is still being referred to as a boy. F does not *say* that Rosalind appears in female dress here but the Duke and Orlando – and Phebe – obviously now first see her as a woman.

122 *bar* stop

127 *holds true contents*. Commentators find the phrase feeble, or incomprehensible, but presumably it means 'if the couples are to remain true to their vows, to what they have alleged to be true'.

128 *cross* trial or affliction

130 *accord* consent

132 *sure together* bound fast

141 *High*. Line 142 suggests that this may mean 'highly' rather than 'true'.

145 *Even daughter*. The phrase is unusual, whether addressed to Celia ('even as a daughter', 'no less than a daughter') or to Rosalind ('and you, my true daughter').

153 *Addressed* gathered, prepared

power armed force

154 *In his own conduct* under his own leadership

157 *religious man* man of some religious function or intent (probably a hermit)

158 *question* discussion

161 *them.* The F reading is 'him', which has been defended on the ground that it was for Duke Senior to restore the lands to the owners if he wished.

163 *engage* pledge

164 *offerest fairly* bringest splendid gifts and offerings

166 *potent* (perhaps not 'powerful' but 'potential': Orlando will inherit it)

167 *do those ends* achieve the aims

170 *shrewd* sharp (a possible reference back to the winter wind and its *icy fang*)

172 *states* status, rank

176 *measures* stately dances (as in line 43 and again in line 190), but with a quibble on *with measure* earlier in the line, where it means 'in good measure', 'liberally'. (In line 172 *measure* has one of its normal modern meanings.)

177 *Sir.* Jaques addresses the Duke, asking his pardon for interrupting and for addressing another directly.

179 *thrown into neglect* rejected as worthless

pompous full of pomp

198 *good wine needs no bush.* This is a proverb ('what is good needs no advertisement') alluding to the vintner's practice of hanging a 'bush' (generally, some ivy) outside his shop.

203 *insinuate with you* subtly work on you and win you over

204 *furnished* dressed (as also in III.2.238)

205 *conjure you* work on you by charms or spells, like a magician

211 *If I were a woman.* The part of Rosalind was, of course, played by a boy – and, characteristically, Shakespeare takes advantage of the fact.

213 *liked* appealed to, pleased

defied disdained

216 *bid me farewell* grant the applause that will allow me to leave the stage in good spirits

AN ACCOUNT OF THE TEXT

As You Like It was first published in the great collection of Shakespeare's plays made after his death, the First Folio of 1623 (hereafter called 'F'). The entry of the play on the Stationers' Register on 4 August 1600 'to be staied' may indicate an intention to prevent publication by others rather than an intention by Shakespeare's company to print it themselves; certainly no publication followed, and the play was duly entered on the Register again on 8 November 1623, among the F plays 'not formerly entred to other men'.

The F text was probably based on an authorial manuscript (or a transcript of one) that had been used in the theatre and then prepared for publication (hence the division into Acts and Scenes). As Charlton Hinman has demonstrated in *The Printing and Proof-Reading of the First Folio of Shakespeare*, the text was set up by no fewer than three different compositors ('B', 'C', and 'D'), probably setting copy simultaneously for much of the time. (The evidence is from differing spelling habits as well as typography.) Accordingly the copy had to be 'cast off' (that is, calculation had to be made in advance of how much printed space a certain amount of the manuscript would take); and if the calculation was wrong, prose could be spun out to look like verse (as seems to have happened in II.6 and III.4) or verse could be printed as prose.

There was some sporadic proof-correcting, on three of the twenty-three pages, as the sheets were being run off; and, in the usual Elizabethan fashion, the incorrect sheets were retained and used as well as those corrected. Hence different copies of F have different readings on three pages (193, 204, and 207), but none of the nine alterations would have required reference to copy. The only two variants of even minor interest are the speech ascriptions of V.1.20 and 21, originally given in error to

Orl. and *Clo.* (Touchstone) and corrected to *Clo.* and *Will.* respectively.

The emendations made in the Second, Third, and Fourth Folios (all in the seventeenth century) are sometimes correct but have no more authority than the emendations of later editors (beginning with Rowe in 1709). Accordingly they are not listed separately here.

COLLATIONS

I

The following emendations of F have been accepted in this edition (the F reading is given after the square bracket, in the original spelling, except that the 'long s' [ſ] has been replaced by 's'). Obvious printer's errors and mislineation (such as that in II.6 and III.4) are not listed; stage directions are treated separately on pages 195–7.

I.1.	103	she] hee
	152	OLIVER] *not in* F
I.2.	51	and hath] hath
	79	CELIA] *Ros.*
	278	Rosalind!] *Rosaline.*
II.1.	49	much] must
II.3.	10	some] seeme
	16	ORLANDO] *not in* F
	29	ORLANDO] *Ad.*
	71	seventeen] seauentie
II.4.	1	weary] merry
	16–17	Ay . . . here: | A . . . talk] *prose in* F
	40	thy wound] they would
	66	you, friend] your friend
	91–2	And . . . place, | And . . . it.] And . . . wages: | I . . . could | Waste . . . it.
II.5.	1	AMIENS (*sings*)] Song (*above the first line*)

6–7 Here ... see | No enemy] *one line in* F

11–13 (*prose*)] I ... prethee more, | I ... song, | As ... more.

15–17 (*prose*)] I ... me, | I ... sing: | Come ... stanzo's?

31–4 (*prose*)] And ... him: | He ... companie: | I ... giue | Heauen ... them. | Come ... come.

43–4 (*prose*)] Ile ... note, | That ... Inuention.

46 JAQUES] *Amy.*

52–3 Here ... see | Gross ... he] *one line in* F

59–60 (*prose*)] And ... Duke, | His ... prepar'd.

II.7. 36 A worthy] O worthie

55 Not to seem] Seeme

101–2 (*prose*)] And ... reason, | I ... dye.

103–4 What ... force, | More ... gentleness.] What ... haue? | Your ... your force | Moue ... gentlenesse.

168–9 Welcome ... burden, | And ... feed] *prose in* F

175 AMIENS (*sings*)] Song.

183 Then hey-ho] *The heigh ho*

III.2. 121 *a desert*] *Desert*

be?] *bee,*

141 *her*] *his*

230 such] forth F1; forth such F2

237 thy] the

246–7 (*prose*)] I ... faith | I ... alone.

248–9 (*prose*)] And ... sake | I ... societie.

348 deifying] defying

III.3. 2 now] how

51 Horns? Even so. Poor men alone?] hornes, euen so poore men alone:

85 (*prose*)] Go ... mee, | And ... thee.

86–95 Come ... *with thee*] Come ... *Audrey*, | We ... baudrey: | Farewel ... Not O ... *Oliuer*, O ... *Oliuer* leaue ... thee: But winde away, bee ... say, I ... with thee.

III.5. 128 I have] Haue

IV.1. 1 me be] me

	17–18	my often] by often
	195	in, it] in, in
IV.2.	10	LORDS] *not in* F
	12–13	Then . . . bear | This burden] *one line in* F
IV.3.	5	*Enter Silvius*] *after* 'brain' *in line 3*
	105	oak] old Oake
V.1.	55	policy] police
V.2.	7	nor her] nor
	13–16	(*prose*)] You . . . consent. | Let . . . I | Inuite . . . followers: | Go . . . looke you, | Heere . . . *Rosalinde.*
V.3.	15	PAGES] *not in* F
	18	ring] *rang*
	33–8	And therefore . . . spring] *follows first stanza* (*lines 15–20*)
V.4.	111	her hand] *his hand*
	112	her bosom] *his bosome*
	117–18	If . . . true, | Why . . . adieu!] *one line in* F
	161	them] him

2

The following emendations of F are plausible enough or popular enough to be worthy of record although they have not been accepted here. The F reading is given first, as modernized in this edition. There have been many other emendations (those of the earlier editions are listed in the New Variorum edition).

I.2.	3	would you yet were merrier] would you yet I were merrier?
	87	the Beu] le Beau
	155	them] her
	232	all promise] promise
	261	taller] shorter (*Rowe*); smaller (*Malone*); lesser (*Spedding*)
I.3.	11	child's father] father's child
	24	try] cry

135 in we] we in
II.1. 5 not] but
50 friend] friends
II.3. 58 meed] need
II.4. 71 travail] travel
II.7. 73 weary] wearer's
III.2. 101 Wintered] Winter
151 Jupiter] pulpiter
III.3. 19 may] it may
46 horn-beasts] horned beasts
III.4. 14 cast] chaste
27 lover] a lover
IV.1. 124 ROSALIND] CELIA
IV.2. 7 LORD] AMIENS
IV.3. 8 did bid] bid
88 sister] forester
156 this] his
V.2.91 or 93 observance] obedience
V.3. 18 the spring time] spring time
41 untuneable] untimeable

3

The following are the principal additions to, or alterations of, the stage directions in F. The F reading is given second, in the original spelling.

I.1. 26 *Adam stands aside*] *not in* F
49 *threatening him*] *not in* F
50 *seizing him by the throat*] *not in* F
59 *coming forward*] *not in* F
88 *Exit Dennis*] *not in* F
I.2. 41 *Enter Touchstone*] *Enter Clowne.*
138 etc. *Duke Frederick*] *Duke* (*similarly elsewhere*)
152 *He stands aside*] *not in* F
199 *Orlando and Charles wrestle*] *Wrastle.*
202 *A shout as Charles is thrown*] *Shout.*

	203	*coming forward*] not in F
	208	*Attendants carry Charles off*] not in F
	218	*Exit Duke, with Lords, Le Beau, and Touchstone*] *Exit Duke.*
	233	*taking a chain from her neck*] not in F
	236	*to Celia*] not in F
	237	*Rosalind and Celia begin to withdraw*] not in F
	245	*To Orlando*] not in F
		Exeunt Rosalind and Celia] *Exit.*
	275	*Exit Le Beau*] not in F
I.3.	87	*Exit Duke, with Lords*] *Exit Duke, &c.*
II.1.	0	*dressed like foresters*] *like Forresters*
II.3.	0	*from opposite sides*] not in F
II.4.	0	*Enter ... Touchstone*] *Enter Rosaline for Ganimed, Celia for Aliena, and Clowne,* alias *Touchstone.*
II.5.	35	ALL TOGETHER (*sing*)] *Song. Altogether heere.*
II.6.	8	*Raising him*] not in F
II.7.	0	*Enter ... outlaws*] *Enter Duke Sen. & Lord, like Out-lawes.*
	136	*Exit*] not in F
III.2.	10	*and Touchstone*] *& Clowne.*
	158	*Exit Touchstone, with Corin*] *Exit.*
	245	*Celia and Rosalind stand back*] not in F
	286	*Exit Jaques*] not in F
	287	*to Celia*] not in F
III.3.	0	*Enter Touchstone and Audrey, followed by Jaques*] *Enter Clowne, Audrey, & Iaques:*
	8, 29, 42	*aside*] not in F
	66	*coming forward*] not in F
	96	*aside*] not in F
III.5.	7	*unobserved*] not in F
	35	*coming forward*] not in F
	66	*to Phebe*] not in F
	67	*to Silvius*] not in F
	69	*To Phebe*] not in F
	74	*To Silvius*] not in F
	80	*Exit Rosalind, with Celia and Corin*] *Exit.*

IV.1. 28 *Going*] *not in* F
29 *as he goes*] *not in* F
IV.2. 0 *Enter Jaques, and Lords dressed as foresters*] *Enter Iaques and Lords, Forresters.*
IV.3. 8 *He gives Rosalind a letter, which she reads*] *not in* F
157 *Rosalind faints*] *not in* F
V.1. 0 *Touchstone and Audrey*] *Clowne and Awdrie.*
V.2. 18 *Exit*] *not in* F
98–113 *to Rosalind* (etc.)] *These (nine) S.D.s are not in* F.
V.3. 0 *Touchstone*] *Clowne*
V.4. 6–16 *to the Duke* (etc.)] *These (four) S.D.s are not in* F.
33 *Touchstone*] *Clowne*
104 *Enter ... themselves*] *Enter Hymen, Rosalind, and Celia.*
113–46 *to the Duke* (etc.)] *These (ten) S.D.s are not in* F.
147 *Second Brother, Jaques de Boys*] *Second Brother.*
183–8 *to the Duke* (etc.)] *These (five) S.D.s are not in* F.
195 *Exeunt all except Rosalind*] *Exit*

THER[illegible]

(I.5) [illegible]

Oliver [illegible]

appears [illegible]

known [illegible]

Touchstone [illegible]

[illegible]

accompaniment [illegible]

THE SONGS

THERE are no early settings of 'Under the greenwood tree' (II.5) or 'Blow, blow, thou winter wind' (II.7). 'O sweet Oliver', from which Touchstone sings fragments (III.3), appears to have been sung to the tune of 'In peascod time', also known as 'The hunt is up'. The version printed below adapts Touchstone's words to the tune.

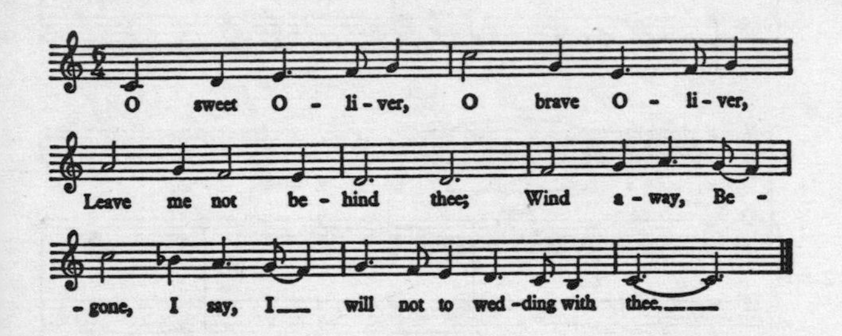

The earliest known setting of 'What shall he have that killed the deer?' (IV.2) is in an arrangement as a catch for four voices made by John Hilton (1599–1657), not published till 1672. The tune may be related to that sung in early performances of the play or it may have been independently composed. It is printed in John H. Long's *Shakespeare's Use of Music* (University of Florida Press, Gainesville, 1955), page 151.

Thomas Morley's well-known setting of 'It was a lover and his lass' (V.3) appeared in his *First Book of Airs, or Little Short Songs* (1600). Its relation to the play is discussed in the Commentary to V.3.15–38. The version given below is from E. H. Fellowes's edition of Morley's book (Stainer & Bell, 1932). The accompaniment is an exact transcription for piano of the lute tablature.

It was a lov - er and his lass, With a
hey, with a ho, and a hey no - ni -
- no, and a hey no - ni no - ni - no,
That o'er the green corn - fields did pass, In
spring time, in spring time, in spring time, the

on - ly pret - ty ring time, When birds do sing, hey
ding a ding a ding, hey ding a ding a ding, hey
ding a ding a ding, Sweet lov - ers love the
spring, In spring time, in spring time, the
on - ly pret - ty ring time, When birds do sing, hey

2

Between the acres of the rye,
With a hey, with a ho, and a hey nonino,
These pretty country fools would lie,
In spring time, the only pretty ring time,
When birds do sing, hey ding a ding a ding,
Sweet lovers love the spring.

3

This carol they began that hour,
With a hey, with a ho, and a hey nonino,
How that a life was but a flower,
In spring time, the only pretty ring time,
When birds do sing, hey ding a ding a ding,
Sweet lovers love the spring.

4

Then pretty lovers take the time,
With a hey, with a ho, and a hey nonino,
For love is crowned with the prime,
In spring time, the only pretty ring time,
When birds do sing, hey ding a ding a ding,
Sweet lovers love the spring.

READ MORE IN PENGUIN

In every corner of the world, on every subject under the sun, Penguin represents quality and variety – the very best in publishing today.

For complete information about books available from Penguin – including Puffins, Penguin Classics and Arkana – and how to order them, write to us at the appropriate address below. Please note that for copyright reasons the selection of books varies from country to country.

In the United Kingdom: Please write to *Dept. EP, Penguin Books Ltd, Bath Road, Harmondsworth, West Drayton, Middlesex UB7 ODA*

In the United States: Please write to *Consumer Sales, Penguin Putnam Inc., P.O. Box 12289 Dept. B, Newark, New Jersey 07101-5289.* VISA and MasterCard holders call 1-800-788-6262 to order Penguin titles

n Canada: Please write to *Penguin Books Canada Ltd, 10 Alcorn Avenue, Suite 300, Toronto, Ontario M4V 3B2*

n Australia: Please write to *Penguin Books Australia Ltd, P.O. Box 257, Ringwood, Victoria 3134*

n New Zealand: Please write to *Penguin Books (NZ) Ltd, Private Bag 102902, North Shore Mail Centre, Auckland 10*

n India: Please write to *Penguin Books India Pvt Ltd, 11 Community Centre, Panchsheel Park, New Delhi 110017*

n the Netherlands: Please write to *Penguin Books Netherlands bv, Postbus 507, NL-1001 AH Amsterdam*

n Germany: Please write to *Penguin Books Deutschland GmbH, Metzlerstrasse 26, 60594 Frankfurt am Main*

n Spain: Please write to *Penguin Books S. A., Bravo Murillo 19, 1° B, 8015 Madrid*

n Italy: Please write to *Penguin Italia s.r.l., Via Benedetto Croce 2, 20094 Corsico, Milano*

n France: Please write to *Penguin France, Le Carré Wilson, 62 rue Benjamin Baillaud, 31500 Toulouse*

n Japan: Please write to *Penguin Books Japan Ltd, Kaneko Building, 3-25 Koraku, Bunkyo-Ku, Tokyo 112*

n South Africa: Please write to *Penguin Books South Africa (Pty) Ltd, Private Bag X14, Parkview, 2122 Johannesburg*

The Royal Shakespeare Company today is probably one of the best known theatre companies in the world, playing regularly to audiences of more than a million people a year. The RSC has three theatres in Stratford-upon-Avon, the Royal Shakespeare Theatre, the Swan Theatre and The Other Place, and two theatres in London's Barbican Centre, the Barbican Theatre and The Pit. The Company also has an annual season in Newcastle-upon-Tyne and regularly undertakes tours throughout the UK and overseas.

Find out more about the RSC and its current repertoire by joining the Company's mailing list. Not only will you receive advance information of all the Company's activities, but also priority booking, special ticket offers, copies of the RSC Magazine and special offers on RSC publications and merchandise.

If you would like to receive details of the Company's work and an application form for the mailing list please write to:

RSC Membership Office
Royal Shakespeare Theatre
FREEPOST
Stratford-upon-Avon
CV37 6BR

or telephone: 01789 205301

READ MORE IN PENGUIN